All about the author...
Sharon Kendrick

When I was told off as a child for making up stories, little did I know that one day I'd earn my living by writing them!

To the horror of my parents, I left school at sixteen and did a bewildering variety of jobs: I was a London DJ (in the now-trendy Primrose Hill!), a decorator and a singer. After that I became a cook, a photographer and eventually a nurse. I waitressed in the south of France, drove an ambulance in Australia and saw lots of beautiful sights, but could never settle down. Everywhere I went I felt like a square peg—until one day I started writing again, and then everything just fell into place.

Today I have the best job in the world—writing passionate romances for Harlequin Books. I like writing stories that are sexy and fast paced, yet packed full of emotion—stories that readers will identify with, that will make them laugh and cry.

My interests are many and varied—chocolate and music, fresh flowers and bubble baths, films and cooking, and trying to keep my home from looking as if someone's burgled it! Simple pleasures—you can't beat them!

I live in Winchester and regularly visit London and Paris. Oh, and I love hearing from my readers all over the world...so I think it's over to you!

With warmest wishes,

Sharon Kendrick (www.sharonkendrick.com)

With special thanks to Anthony Maskell for his unflappable emergency rescue (they should call you Thunderbird!), David Carter for averting my breakdown (though sadly not the mechanical one!) and that most eminent of historians Richard (Dick! Blaine!) for his genial hospitality.

Of course, we must not forget the beauty that is Cascob…and Guy Black.

HARLEQUIN®
Presents~

Welcome to a month of fantastic reading, brought to you by Harlequin Presents!

For your pleasure is the first book of Sandra Marton's new THE BILLIONAIRES' BRIDES trilogy, *The Italian Prince's Pregnant Bride*, where Prince Nicolo Barbieri acquires Aimee Black, who, it seems, is pregnant with Nicolo's baby! Then favorite author Lynne Graham brings you a gorgeous Greek in *The Petrakos Bride*, where Maddie comes face-to-face again with her tycoon idol....

In *His Private Mistress* by Chantelle Shaw, Italian racing driver Rafael is determined to make Eden his mistress once more...while in *One-Night Baby* by Susan Stephens, another Italian knows nothing of the secret Kate is hiding from their one night together. If a sheikh is what gets your heart thumping, Annie West brings you *For the Sheikh's Pleasure*, where Sheikh Arik is determined to get Rosalie to open up to receive the loving that only *he* can give her! In *The Brazilian's Blackmail Bargain* by Abby Green, Caleb makes Maggie an offer she just can't refuse. And finally Lindsay Armstrong's *The Rich Man's Virgin* tells the story of a fiercely independent woman who finds she's pregnant by a powerful millionaire. Look out for more brilliant books next month!

Sharon Kendrick
THE BILLIONAIRE BODYGUARD

TORONTO • NEW YORK • LONDON
AMSTERDAM • PARIS • SYDNEY • HAMBURG
STOCKHOLM • ATHENS • TOKYO • MILAN • MADRID
PRAGUE • WARSAW • BUDAPEST • AUCKLAND

ISBN-13: 978-0-373-18878-9
ISBN-10:   0-373-18878-1

THE BILLIONAIRE BODYGUARD

First North American Publication 2007.

Copyright © 2004 by Sharon Kendrick.

This edition published by arrangement with Harlequin Books S.A.

® and TM are trademarks of the publisher. Trademarks indicated with
® are registered in the United States Patent and Trademark Office, the
Canadian Trade Marks Office and in other countries.

www.eHarlequin.com

Printed in U.S.A.

CHAPTER ONE

HE DIDN'T say much, but maybe that was best. There was nothing worse than a driver who talked.

Keri settled back in the soft leather seat of the luxury car and stared at the back of the man in the driving seat in front of her. No, definitely no talker he—more the strong, silent type. Very strong—judging by the broad set of those shoulders—and very definitely silent. There had been little more than a nod when he had picked her up from her London flat early that morning, and very little since.

Keri shivered. Outside the snowflakes continued to flurry down—big, fat, splodgy things which melted on your cheeks and clung like stubborn confetti to your hair.

She pulled her sheepskin coat tighter and huddled into it. 'Brrr! Could you turn the heater up a little? I'm absolutely freezing.'

His eyes intently fixed on the road ahead, Jay flicked a switch. 'Can do.'

'And would you mind putting your foot down? I want to get back to London some time tonight.'

'I'll do my best,' he said equably.

He would drive only as fast as conditions demanded, no more and no less. Jay's face was hidden, but he flicked a glance at the rearview mirror to see the model sliding a pair of fur-lined gloves over her long fingers. If she *had* been able to see him she would have seen the unmistakable look of irritation on his face. Not that his irritation would have bothered her, of course—even if she had picked it up. He was simply the driver—employed to cater to her every whim and keep close watch on the priceless chandelier of a necklace which had been dripping exquisite diamonds from her long, pale neck during one of the coldest afternoons of the year.

He had watched while the stylists and the photographers and all their assistants had fussed round her, and had observed her blank, almost bored look of compliance as she had let them. He had been pretty bored himself, if the truth were known. Watching a magazine-shoot seemed to involve one hell of a lot of waiting around. The waiting he could deal with, if there was a good reason for it, but this had seemed like a complete waste of time.

To Jay, it had seemed crazy that a woman would agree to wear a flimsy evening dress outdoors on a bitterly icy day. Surely they could have recreated a winter scene inside the warmth and comfort of a studio, and made his job easier?

And then he had seen the Polaroids, and suddenly he had understood. Before the camera she had come alive—and how. He had given a long, low whistle and the photographer's assistant had flashed him a conspiratorial smile.

'Gorgeous, isn't she?'

Jay had studied them. Sure, she was exquisite—just like the diamonds themselves, if you liked diamonds, which personally he didn't. Framed by the sooty fall of her loose hair, her face was pale as a dusting of frost, her eyes as dark as the bare charcoal branches of the trees. Her lips were full and red—painted crimson, like rich ruby wine—and they parted into a shape of sheer, moist provocation. The thin silver gown had added to the wintry feel of the photograph, and it had clung like sparkling hoar-frost to her body, to the firm, high breasts and the curving bottom.

But she'd looked as if she had been made from ice, or wax—too perfect to be true and not real at all. If you pricked a woman like that, would she bleed? he wondered. If you made love to her, would she cry out in wild, uninhibited passion—or would she just smooth down that perfect hair and flick it back over her shoulders?

'She's okay,' he had drawled, and the assistant had given him another understanding smile.

'I know what you mean.' He'd shrugged. 'Not just a case of out of our league—she's probably never even heard of our league!'

Jay had nodded and turned away, not bothering to correct him—the day he decided a woman was out of his league would be the day he failed to draw breath. He was here to do a job and get away as soon as possible. He shouldn't even have been there in the first place, and he had a date that night with a cool dream of a blonde he had been fighting off without quite knowing why—only tonight he had decided that maybe it was time to throw in the towel.

A slow smile of anticipation curved his mouth.

'How long, do you think?'

The model's voice cut into thoughts which were just

threatening to get erotic, and her question didn't really help.

'How long is what?' he questioned.

Keri sighed. It had been a long, long day and, if the truth were known, she would have liked nothing more than to go home to a hot bath and then curl herself up with a good book instead of go out on a dinner date. Not that dinner with David would be anything other than enjoyable—it always was. True, he didn't set her pulses on fire, but he knew that and he didn't mind a bit. Well, that was what he said—but Keri couldn't help wondering if, deep down, he was quietly working on a campaign to make her change her mind. And she wouldn't, of course. David fell firmly into the category of friend and was stuck there, and that was probably best. Lovers—at least in Keri's limited experience—tended to be bad news.

'I was asking how long it will take us to get back to London.'

Jay narrowed his eyes at the road ahead. The snow was getting heavier now. The skies were pale grey, so pale that it was impossible to see where the falling, swirling snow ended and the sky began. Trees loomed up as they passed—skeletal brooms so inhospitable that you could not imagine them ever bearing fruit or leaves or blossoms.

It was tempting to say that if she hadn't wasted so much time then they would be well on their way now, but he didn't. It wasn't the job of the driver to offer anything in the way of opinions, which took more than a little self-restraint on his part.

'Difficult to say,' he murmured. 'Depends.'

'On what?' Something about that lazy, drawled air of assurance was making her prickly. What kind of driver was he, anyway, if he couldn't throw in a rough estimate of their time of arrival?

He heard the faintly impatient note in her voice and hid a smile. He had forgotten what it was like to be subordinate—to have people tell you what to do and to ask you questions and expect you to answer, just as if you were some kind of machine.

'On how bad this snow gets,' he said, frowning suddenly as he felt the treacherous slide of the front wheels. He slowed right down.

Keri stared out of the window. 'It doesn't look that bad to me.'

'You think so?' he murmured. 'Well, that's okay, then.'

He had a faint, almost American drawl, and for a moment she thought she detected a mocking note of humour underpinning it. Suspiciously, Keri stared at the unmoving set of his broad shoulders. Was he making fun of her?

Through a gap in the thick curtain of dark fringe which flopped into her eyes Jay could see the tiny frown which pleated the smooth, pale perfection of her forehead. 'Would you like the radio on?' he questioned, as soothingly as he would to a maiden aunt who was in danger of becoming fractious.

He was making her feel...uncomfortable, and she couldn't quite put her finger on why. 'Actually,' said Keri, very deliberately, 'what I would really like is to get some sleep, so if you wouldn't mind...?'

'Sure. No problem.' Jay hid a smile which vanished

as he drove further into the winter dusk. The flakes of snow had changed from being the innocent ones of storybook pictures—now they were small, and he knew that they would have the bite of ice behind them. The wind was gusting them into bitter white flurries so that they looked like swarms of white bees.

He glanced in the mirror again. She had fallen asleep. Her head had fallen back and her hair was spread out behind it, like a shiny black pillow. The blanket had slipped down and the slit in her skirt meant that her long legs were sprawled out—pretty much the longest legs he had ever seen on a woman. Legs like that could wrap themselves round a man's neck like a deadly snake. Deliberately, Jay averted his eyes from their coltish display and from the tantalising glimpse of lacy stocking-top. This drive was going to take longer than he had anticipated—far better she slept than distract him.

But the weather was distraction enough. The narrow lanes became more precarious by the second, with the snow falling heavier and heavier, and as night closed in the darkness hid the fall from sight and the car began to slow as it encountered the first drifts.

He knew way before it happened that things were going to get bad—really bad. Instinct told him that, coupled with the experience of having lived in some of the most God-awful conditions known to man.

His windscreen wipers were flicking dementedly, but still it was like gazing into an icy abyss. The road dipped slightly, and he eased his foot back. A dip was good. Slopes ran down into hollows and hollows were where you found people, and they built houses which equalled shelter, and he suspected that they very soon they might need shelter... Except that this was pretty desolate countryside. Unspoiled, he guessed. Chosen for its beauty and its very isolation.

He flicked the light on briefly, to glance down at the map, and then squinted his eyes as the car passed the darkened bulk of a building. Some way after that, Jay realised that he no longer had a choice, and braked. Hard.

The jerk of the car woke her, and Keri opened her eyes, caught in that warm half-world between waking and sleeping. She yawned. 'Where are we?' she questioned sleepily.

'In the middle of nowhere,' he answered succinctly. 'Take a look for yourself.'

The sound of the low, tough masculine voice shook her right out of her reverie, and for a moment it startled her, until she realised where she was. She looked out of the window, and then blinked. He wasn't joking.

While she had been sleeping the snowy landscape had been transformed into one which was now unrecognisable. Night had closed in, and with it the snow. Everything was black and white, like a photographic negative, and it would have been beautiful if it didn't look so...*forbidding*. And they were in the middle of it. Of nowhere, as he had said. 'Why have you stopped?' she asked.

Why do you think I've stopped? 'Because the fall is heavy here.'

'Well, how long is it going to take us to get back now?'

Jay shot another glance out, and then looked in the mirror at her beautiful perplexed face. It was clear from her question that she had no idea how bad it was, and he was going to have to break it to her. Gently.

'If it carries on like this there's no way we're going to make it back at all, at least not tonight—we'll be lucky if we make it as far as the nearest village.'

This was sounding like something out of a bad movie. 'But I don't want to go to a village!' she exclaimed. 'I want to go to home!'

I want. I want. He supposed a woman like that spent all her time getting exactly what it was she wanted. Well, not tonight. 'You and me both, sweetheart,' he said grimly. 'But I'll settle for what I can take.'

She let the sweetheart bit go. Now was not the time to get frosty because he was being over-familiar. 'Can't you just drive on?'

He pressed cautiously on the accelerator, then eased his foot off. 'Nope. We're stuck.'

Keri sat bolt upright. 'What do you mean?'

What the hell do you think I mean? 'Like I said, we're stuck. There are drifts in the road. Snowdrifts. And they're underpacked with ice. It's a potentially lethal situation.'

Keri briefly shut her eyes. *Please tell me this isn't happening.* She opened them again. 'Couldn't you have predicted this might happen and taken a different route?'

He might have let it go, but something in her accusation made his blood simmer. 'There *is* no alternative route—not out of that God-forsaken field they chose for the shoot—and, if you recall, I asked you three times to hurry up. I said that I didn't like the look of the sky. But you were too busy being fawned over by a load of luvvies to pay much attention to what I was saying.'

Was he *criticising* her? 'I was just doing my job!'

'And I'm *trying* to do mine,' he said darkly. 'Which is dealing with the situation as it is, not wasting time by casting around for recriminations!'

Keri stared at the back of his dark head, feeling like a tennis-player who had been wrong-footed. And the most annoying thing of all was that he was right. He might have an arrogant, almost insolent way of expressing himself, but she could see his logic. 'So what do you suggest we do?' she questioned coolly.

By *we* he guessed she meant *him*. 'I guess we find some shelter.'

'No.' Keri shook her head. What did he think—that she was going to book into a hotel for the night? With *him*? 'I don't think you understand—I have to be back in London. Tonight.' She eyed his muscular frame hopefully. 'Can't you dig us out?'

'With a spare snow-plough?' Jay smiled. 'I don't think *you* understand, sweetheart—even if I dug us out, it would only be a temporary measure. This road is impassable.'

She felt a momentary flare of panic, until reason reasserted itself. 'You can't know that!'

He wasn't about to start explaining that he had seen snow and ice in pretty much all its guises. The empty bleached horizons of arctic wastes which made this particular snow scene look like a benign Christmas card. Or swimming beneath polar ice-caps and wondering if your blood had frozen solid in your veins, wetsuit or no wetsuit. Men trapped…lost…never to be heard of again.

A hard note entered his voice. 'Oh, but I can—it's my job to know.' He turned off the ignition, and turned round and shrugged. 'Sorry, but that's the way it is.'

She opened her mouth to reply, but the words froze on her lips as she met his eyes for the first time—hard, glittering eyes which took her breath away, and it was a long time since a man had done that. It was the first time she had looked at him properly, but then you never really looked at a driver, did you? They were part of the fixtures and fittings, part of the car itself—or at least they were supposed to be. She sucked in a dry gulp of air, confused by the sudden pounding of her heart, as if it was trying to remind her that it still existed. Lord alive, what was a man like this doing driving a car for a living?

His face was chiselled—all hard and lean angles—which seemed at odds with the lush, sensual curve of his upper lip. In the low light she couldn't make out the colour of his slanting eyes, but she could appreciate the feathery forest of lashes which gave them such an enigmatic look, and she had been modelling for long enough to know that cheekbones like that were rare.

He was, quite simply, *gorgeous*.

Jay noted the dilation of her eyes with something approaching wry amusement and then put it out of his mind. This was business, not pleasure—and even if it had been he wasn't into spoiled, pretty girls who expected everyone to jump when they spoke.

'So we could stay here all night,' he said pleasantly. 'Keep the engine running and wait until morning and hope it gets better.'

Spend the night in the car? 'Are you *serious*?'

'Completely.' He would keep awake quite easily—he had had a lifetime's experience of waiting for the first faint glow of a winter dawn.

There was something so unequivocal about that one clipped-out word that Keri began to realise that he meant it. But surely there was something they could do? This was England, for heaven's sake—not the Rocky Mountains!

'We must be able to phone for help.' She began to fish around in her handbag. 'I have a mobile here somewhere.'

His own was snug in his pocket—did she really think he hadn't thought of that? 'Sure, go ahead,' he murmured. 'Call the emergency services and tell them we're in trouble.'

She knew just from the tone of his voice that there would be no signal, but stubborn pride made her jab at the buttons with frustration coupled with rising panic.

'No luck?' he questioned sardonically.

Her hand was shaking, but she put the phone back in her handbag with as much dignity as possible. 'So we really are stuck,' she said flatly.

'Looks like it.' Her eyes looked huge and dark, all wide and appealing in her pale, heart-shaped face—designed by nature to provoke protectiveness in a man.

And nature was a funny thing, he mused—a nose, two eyes and a mouth could be arranged in such a way to transform a face from the ordinary into the exquisite. Luck of the draw, like so much else in life. 'Listen,' he drawled, 'I thought I could make out a building a little way back. It makes far more sense to head for that. I'll go and investigate.'

The thought of being left here all alone made her feel even worse. What if he disappeared into the cold and snowy night and never came back again? What if someone came along? It wasn't much of a contest, but on balance she'd probably be much safer with him than staying here without him. He might be a little lacking in the respect department, but at least he seemed to know what he was doing. 'No, I don't want you leaving me here,' she said. 'I'm coming with you.'

His eyes flickered over her leather boots. They were good, soft, waterproof leather, but heels like that weren't made for walking. And neither, by the look of it, was she. He raised his eyebrows. 'Not exactly dressed for it, are you?'

'Well, I wasn't expecting to have to go for a *hike*!'

His eyes narrowed. 'Ever skied?'

Keri laughed. 'With my job? You're kidding—skiing is classified as a dangerous sport and therefore frowned on.'

Pretty restrictive job, he thought. 'Well, you're sure you're up to it?'

'I can manage,' she said stubbornly.

He supposed that there was no choice but to let her try. 'You'll have to—because there's no way I'm carrying you.' His eyes mocked her again as he saw her lips part, and he realised that he was lying. Of course he would carry her, just the way he had been conditioned to do. Men would walk miles across any terrain for a woman who looked like that. 'Button up your coat,' he said roughly. 'And put your gloves back on.'

She opened her mouth to ask him to please stop addressing her as he would an idiot, but something about the set of his mouth told her that the dynamics had subtly changed and he was no longer *just* the driver. It was indefinable but unmistakable from his body language that suddenly he was in charge. And she wasn't used to that either.

'Hat?' he drawled.

She shook her head and he reached in the glove compartment for a beanie and handed it to her.

'Put your hair up,' he instructed. 'And then put this on.'

'Won't you need it yourself?'

'You need it more,' he stated. 'You're a woman.'

She thought about making some clever remark about equality, but something cool and implacable in his eyes told her not to bother, as if he didn't really care *what* she thought. For a woman used to men hanging on her every word, it was certainly a change.

He got out and came round and opened the door for her, pulling it back with difficulty, for snow was piled up against it.

'Be careful,' he warned. 'It's cold and it's deep. Just follow me, okay? Close as you can and quickly as you can. And do exactly as I tell you.'

It was most definitely an order.

He seemed to know exactly where he was going,

even though Keri could barely make out what was lane or field or sky or hedge. She panted slightly as she stumbled into the blinding whiteness. It was an effort to keep up with him and he kept having to stop, turning to look at her, the slanting eyes narrowing.

'You okay?'

She nodded. 'I'm being slow, aren't I?'

You're a woman, and you aren't trained up for this kind of stuff. 'Don't worry about it. Fingers not freezing too badly?'

'Wh-what fingers are they?' She shivered.

He laughed then, an unexpected and oddly musical sound, and his breath made frozen clouds in the air. 'Not long now,' he promised softly.

As she teetered behind him she wondered how he could be so sure. Swirling flakes of snow flew against her face, shooting into her eyes and melting on her lips. The boots she had thought comfortable were only so in the context of a short stroll down a London street. Her feet felt as if they had been jammed into sardine cans and her toes were beginning to ache and to burn. And her fingers *were* freezing—so cold that she couldn't feel them any more.

She had never been so aware of her body in such an aching and uncomfortable way, and with the unfamiliar feelings of physical discomfort came an equally unfamiliar fear. What if they *couldn't* find the place he had claimed he had seen? Hadn't she read newspaper reports of people freezing to death, or getting lost in conditions not unlike this?

A shiver quite unconnected to the cold ran through her. Why hadn't they just waited in the car and sat it out until morning? At least they would have been easily found there. She bit her lip hard, but scarcely felt it, then he stopped suddenly.

'Here!' he said, and a note of satisfaction deepened his voice into a throaty growl. 'I knew it!'

Keri peered ahead, her breath a painful, icy gasp which shot from her lungs. 'What is it?' she questioned weakly.

'Shelter!'

As she came alongside it, it loomed up before her like a spectre. It didn't look either warm or welcoming. It was a very tall building—almost like a small church—and the path leading up to it was banked high with snow. There was no light whatsoever, and the high windows were uncurtained, but at least it was shelter.

And Keri did what any woman would do under the circumstances.

She burst into tears.

CHAPTER TWO

JAY narrowed his eyes and gave her a quick, assessing look. How like a woman! The Canadians had at least five different descriptions for snow; the Icelanders countless more—and so it was with women and their tears. They cried at the drop of a hat, for all kind of reasons, and it rarely meant anything serious. And these, he surmised, were simply tears of relief.

He ignored them.

'There's nobody home,' he said, half to himself. If indeed it *was* somebody's home.

The tears had taken her off guard. She couldn't remember the last time she had cried, for that was one thing her job *had* given her, in spades—the ability to hide her feelings behind a bright, professional smile. She supposed she should be grateful that he hadn't drawn attention to them, yet perversely she felt short-changed because he hadn't attempted to comfort her— even in a small way—and she scrubbed at the corners of her eyes rather defensively, with a frozen fist. 'How can you tell?' she sniffed.

Explaining would take longer than going through the motions, and so he began to pound at the door with a loud fist. He waited, but, as he had known, the place was empty.

'Stand back,' he said tersely.

'Why?'

'Because I'm going to have to get us inside.'

Keri eyed the door, which was made of strong, heavy oak. 'You're planning to kick the door in, are you?' she asked disbelievingly.

He shook his head, half tempted to give a macho display of strength just to show her. 'No, I'll jimmy the lock instead.'

'*J-jimmy the lock?*' It wasn't an expression she was familiar with, but she could work out what he meant. Alarmed, Keri took a step back and very nearly lost her balance, but he didn't appear to have noticed that either. 'You can't do that! That's called breaking and entering!'

He shot her one impatient glance. 'And what do you suggest?' he questioned coolly. 'That we stand here all night and freeze to death just to have our good citizen medals awarded to us?'

'No, of course I—'

'Then just shut up for a minute and let me concentrate, will you?'

This was an order verging on the simply rude, but Keri didn't have time to be indignant, because, to her astonishment, he produced what looked like a screwdriver from the pocket of his flying jacket, leaving her wondering slightly hysterically if it was a necessary job requirement for all drivers to have house-breaking skills. She dug her gloved hands deep into the pockets of her coat, and with chattering teeth prepared for a long wait.

But with astonishing speed he was soon opening the front door, a small smile playing at the corners of his mouth as he saw her look of horror.

'You look surprised,' he commented.

'Surprise isn't quite the right word—how the hell did you manage to do it so quickly?' she demanded as she stepped inside and he shut the door firmly behind her.

'You don't want to know,' he drawled. 'Just put it down as one of many skills I have.'

Oh, great! What kind of a maniac had she found herself marooned with? A thief? Or worse?

She eyed him with apprehension, but he was looking around him, his face raised slightly, almost like an animal which had found itself in a new and potentially hostile terrain, his hard body tensed and watchful.

Jay was enjoying himself, he realised. He had forgotten what it was like to live on his wits, to cope with the unexpected, to use his instincts and his strength again. It had been a long time. Too long. 'Nobody lives here,' he said softly. 'At least, not all the time.'

'How can you tell?'

'Because it's cold—really cold. And there's no smell—when a place is inhabited people always leave a scent around.' He stared down at the floor, where the shadowed outline of untouched post lay. 'But it's more than that—it's a feeling. A place that isn't lived in feels lonely.'

Lonely…yes—quite apart from its geographical isolation, the house had a lonely feel. And Keri knew exactly what that meant—you could have the busiest life in the world, but inside you could sometimes feel achingly lonely.

'So here we are,' he said softly. Alone and stranded

in a beautiful house with a beautiful woman. An unexpected perk.

His voice had dipped, and deepened, and Keri stared at him, the reality of their situation suddenly hitting her for the first time. It was just her and him. As her eyes became more accustomed to the gloom she started to become aware of him in a way which was too vivid and confusing. Not as someone employed by the company who had commissioned the photo-shoot, but as something quite different.

As a man.

The first impression she had had in the car had been the correct one—he was spectacular. Very tall—taller than she was, and that didn't happen too often either, because Keri was tall for a woman—models usually were. But it wasn't just his height which she was inexplicably finding so intimidating, it was something much more subtle, more dangerous, and it was all to do with the almost tangible masculinity radiating off him, and the raw, feral heat which seemed to make a mockery of the weather outside.

Keri swallowed, and inside her gloves the palms of her hands began to grow clammy, and maybe the place had just telescoped in on itself, because right now it felt small and claustrophobic, even though the hall was high and spacious. And perhaps he felt it too, because he reached out a hand towards the light switch.

'Let's see if we can throw a little light on the... damn!'

'What's the matter?'

'Should have guessed. No power.' He swore quietly underneath his breath and pulled a lighter out of his pocket, flicking the lid off and sliding his thumb down over the wheel. His face was startlingly illuminated by the bright flare.

'You don't happen to have a white rabbit in your pocket, too?' she questioned, but she noticed that her voice sounded high and rather wobbly.

He looked her up and down. 'You okay?'

Well, up until he had produced the lighter she had been fine, under the circumstances. Tearstained, cold and slightly shell-shocked, true, but more than a little relieved to be inside—if not exactly in the warm, then at least in the dry. But the more she saw of him, the more she realised that the first impression she had got of him in the shadowed recess of the car wasn't strictly accurate.

She had thought that he was good-looking, but she had been wrong. Good-looking implied something that was attractive on the surface but with little real depth to it, like lots of the male models she knew. Whereas this man...

Her breath suddenly caught in her throat.

The flare from the lighter threw deep shadows beneath the high cheekbones and his eyes glittered with a cold, intelligent gleam. She became aware of a strength that came from within, as well as from the deeply defined muscular build. He looked confident and unshakable, while she, on the other hand, was left feeling slightly dazed.

'I'm...I'm fine,' she managed, thinking that she had to pull herself together. It looked as if they might be here for some time—and if that were the case then she quickly needed to establish some kind of neutral re-

lationship between them. So that they both knew
where they were. They needed boundaries so that they
wouldn't step over them. She mustn't think of him as
a man. He's the driver of your car, for heaven's sake,
Keri! And a burly security guard who has been employed to...to...

'Oh, my God!' she exclaimed.

He frowned. 'What is it?'

'The necklace! You're supposed to be guarding the
necklace!'

His mouth curved into a disapproving line. 'Well,
isn't that just like a woman? Save them from the ex-
tremes, find them shelter and safety, and all they can
think of is damned diamonds!'

He dug his other hand in his pocket and indolently
pulled out the gems so that they fell sinuously over
his hand, where they glittered and sparkled with pure
ice-fire against the tanned dark skin of his hand.
'There?' He sent her a mocking look. 'Happy now?'

Keri felt anything but. She was used to deference
and adoration—she certainly wasn't used to men who
behaved with such unashamed masculine *swagger*.
Who clipped out orders and broke into strange houses
with ease and didn't seem a bit bothered by it. 'You
must be the happy one,' she observed. 'Happy you
didn't lose them—after all, it's more than your job's
worth!'

Jay smiled. It was a remark designed to put him
firmly in his place; but Miss Beauty would soon dis-
cover that he was a man who did not fit into traditional
slots. He slid the gems back negligently into his
pocket. 'That's right,' he agreed innocently. 'Can't

have them thinking I've skipped to pawn them on the black market, can we? Now, let's see if we can find a candle somewhere. We need to get a fire lit, but first I guess we'd better check out the rest of the house.'

Her teeth were chattering. 'With a view to finding— what, exactly?'

A dark sense of humour made him consider making a joke about corpses, but in view of the tears he thought he'd better not try. The trouble with women was that they always let their imaginations run away with them.

'With a view, sweetheart, to seeing what luxuries this place has to offer.'

There—he was doing it again. 'I am *not* your sweet-heart.'

Touchy. 'Well, then, I guess we'd better introduce ourselves,' he drawled. 'Since I don't even know your name.'

How bizarre it seemed, to be introducing themselves like this. As if all the normal rules of social intercourse had been turned upside down and re-invented. Into what? 'Keri.' She hesitated. 'And I, er, I don't know yours either.'

He could hear her skating round the edges of asking him, unsure whether or not it was 'appropriate' to be on first-name terms with him. She didn't know how to react to the situation, he thought with wry amuse-ment. Or to him. Take her out of her gilded cage and she probably didn't know how to fly properly! Maybe his first impression of a woman who would not bleed or love with vigour and passion had been the right one all along. 'It's Linur,' he said sardonically. 'Jay Linur.'

It was an unusual name, maybe that was why it suited him. Again, she felt the need to re-establish boundaries. 'Are you...American?'

He knew exactly what she was trying to do. That vaguely interested, vaguely patronising tone. His eyes sparked. 'Fascinating as my name must be to you,' he drawled, 'I'm freezing my bones off—so why don't we postpone the discussion until we've had a look around? Want to go and explore?'

'Do I have a choice?'

'Well, I guess we *could* stand around here and make polite conversation.'

'I'd hate to put you under any pressure,' she said sweetly. 'The strain of that might prove too much for you.'

He gave a brief smile. 'It just might,' he agreed silkily, but the subtle taunt set his pulse racing almost as much as the rose-petalled pout of her lips.

He seemed to show no fear, and she tried not to feel any either—yet who knew what they might find in this strange, empty place? Keri stayed as close to him as was possible without actually touching.

Illuminated only by the small flicker from the lighter, he led the way to what was obviously a kitchen—although by no stretch of the imagination did it resemble any kitchen Keri had ever seen before.

From the doorway, she surveyed the faint shape of ancient-looking appliances.

'I'm going to hunt around for some candles,' he said softly. 'Wait here.'

I'm not going anywhere because I can't, she thought rather desperately, as she watched him disappear into the gloom. He doesn't need me at all, but I need him. She could hear him opening drawers and cupboards, and the clatter of china as he hunted around. He suddenly made a small yelp of satisfaction, and when he reappeared it was with two lit candles waxed to saucers. He handed her one, the reflection of the flame flickering in his eyes.

'Hold it steady,' he instructed.

'I'm just about capable of carrying a candle!'

His mocking eyes seemed to doubt her, but he didn't retaliate.

'Come on—we'll look upstairs first.'

There were three bedrooms, but they looked ghostly and unreal, for the beds were stripped bare of all linen and there was no sign that they had been slept in.

'I feel like Goldilocks,' whispered Keri in a hollow voice. 'Any minute now and we'll bump into one of the three bears.'

'I've never been particularly fond of porridge,' he murmured. 'Come on, there's no point hanging around here.'

There was an archaic-looking bathroom, with a huge free standing bath.

Jay went over to the cistern and flushed the lavatory, and a great whooshing sound made Keri start.

'Well, that's something,' he said drily.

Thank God it was dark or he might have seen her blush—but Keri had never lived with anyone except for her family, and this was one more thing which felt too uncomfortably intimate.

They went back downstairs and moved in the opposite direction from the kitchen. Jay opened a door and looked down into pitch blackness.

'Cellar,' he said succinctly. 'Want to explore?'

'I think I'll pass on that.'

On the other side of the hall was a heavy oak, door and Jay pushed it open, waiting for a moment while the candle flame stopped guttering.

'Come over here, Keri,' he said softly, his words edged with an odd, almost excited note. 'And look at this.'

Keri went down the step and followed the direction of his gaze. 'Oh, my word,' she breathed. 'I feel like Aladdin.'

'Yeah.' His voice was thoughtful. 'I know what you mean.'

It was like stumbling unawares upon a treasure trove—a gloriously old and elegant room which looked as though it belonged to another age. Jay held the candle aloft and Keri could see that it was as high as four men—with a pointed raftered ceiling made out of dark, wooden beams—and the room itself was so big that she could not see the edges.

'Where are we?' she said. 'What is this place?'

He was busy taking more candles from his pocket and lighting them, placing one on the mantelpiece and one on a low table in front of the empty grate. 'I don't know, and right at this moment I really don't care.'

It was amazing what a little light did, and as more of it appeared so did the room, and the dark, threatening shadows were banished and forgotten as she looked around. It was beautiful.

There were high, arched windows and a mighty fireplace, with two enormously long sofas sprawled at right-angles beside it. In one corner stood a piano, and there were books crammed into shelves on one wall and pictures on the walls.

'It looks almost like a church,' she whispered.

'Why are you whispering?' he asked, in a normal voice, and the sound seemed to shatter through the air.

'I don't know. Anyway, you were whispering too!' Keri's teeth began to chatter as the icy temperature began to register on her already chilled skin. 'B-but wh-wherever or whatever this place is, it's even c-colder here than it is outside.'

'Yeah.' He crouched down beside the fireplace, an old-fashioned type he had never seen before and big enough to roast an ox in. 'So why don't I light this, and you go and have a scout about—see what kind of supplies there are?' She was looking at him blankly, and he let out an impatient sigh as he began to pull some kindling towards him. 'Sustenance,' he explained. 'Food, drink, coffee, a spare suckling pig—anything.'

Keri eyed the darkness warily. 'On my own?'

He glanced up. Clearly she was a woman to whom the word 'initiative' was a stranger. 'You mean you want me to come and hold your hand for you?'

'No, of course not,' she said stiffly.

'There's nothing to be afraid of.' His voice softened by a fraction. 'Here, take a candle with you.'

'Well, I'm hardly going to feel my way out there in the dark!' She lifted her hand to her head. 'But before I do anything, I'm getting rid of this hat.'

His eyes narrowed as she pulled the snow-damp

beanie off, shaking her hair out so that it fell and splayed in night-dark glossy tendrils before falling down over the soft curves of her breasts. It was a captivating movement, as elegant as a dancer, and he wondered whether it just came naturally or if she'd learnt it from her modelling career. Keep your mind on the job, he told himself.

Except that the job he had set out to do was turning into something quite different. He sat back on his haunches and his eyes travelled up the endless length of her legs. He felt a pulse beat deep in his groin—an instinctive reaction to a beautiful woman. God, it had been a long time. 'Run along now,' he said softly. 'My throat is parched.'

Run along? *Run along?* 'Don't talk to me that way,' she said in a low voice.

He looked up. 'What way is that?'

As though he were some kind of caveman and she was the little woman, scurrying away with whatever he'd successfully hunted that day. Though when she stopped to think about it there was something pretty primitive about the deft way he seemed to be constructing the fire.

'You know *exactly* what way I'm talking about!'

'You mean you just can't cope with a man unless he's paying homage to you, is that it?'

'Don't put words into my mouth!'

If her feet hadn't been hurting so much, and if she hadn't been afraid that the candle might go out, then Keri might have flounced out of the room. But Jay Linur didn't seem like the kind of man who would be impressed by any kind of flouncing, and so she made do with walking, her back perfectly straight, her head held very high.

She made her way back to the kitchen and looked around. It didn't look very hopeful. An ancient old oven which looked as though it had seen better days. A big, scrubbed wooden table. And that was about it. A cupboard yielded little more than a couple of tins, and a box of dusty old teabags which had clearly seen better days.

She filled the kettle with water, but the kettle wouldn't work, and she remembered why and went back into the huge room, where he had managed to coax a tiny flame from the fire.

He looked up. 'What is it?'

'The kettle won't work! There's no electricity—remember?'

He stared at her consideringly. 'How about gas?' He raised his eyebrows questioningly and then shook his head. 'I don't believe it—you haven't even bothered to check, have you?'

She felt like telling him that she was a model, not a girl guide. And that she didn't even *want* a hot drink, and that if he *did* then he could jolly well go and make it himself. But there was something so forbidding about the expression on his face that she decided against it. Being stuck here with him was like a nightmare come true, but Keri suspected that it would be even more of a nightmare if he *wasn't* here.

'No,' she admitted reluctantly.

'Then I suggest you go and try again.'

He was doing it again—dismissing her as if she was a schoolgirl. This had to be addressed some time, and maybe it was best she did it now. 'Did anyone ever tell you that you are distinctly lacking in the charm department?'

'Oh.' There was a pause. 'Is it charm you want you want from me, then, Keri?'

The question threw her as much as the smoky look of challenge in his eyes and the silky note of caress in his voice, and suddenly she became aware of a whispering of unwelcome sensation, too nebulous to define. Almost as if... She shook her head to deny it and gave him her coolest smile, the kind which could intimidate most men—a frosty and distancing kind of smile. 'Not at all—but if you could hold back on the arrogant, macho, bossing-me-around kind of behaviour, I'd be very grateful.'

He raised his eyebrows laconically. 'You don't like it?'

'Show me a woman who does!'

'I could show you legions,' he observed softly, thinking of two in particular.

'Not *this* woman!'

He watched her wiggle out of the room in that sinful leather skirt, imagining its softness as it swished against her thighs.

In the kitchen, Keri gingerly scouted around, trying to rid herself of that strange, tingly sensation which was making her feel almost light-headed—as if her blood had suddenly come to life in her veins, making her acutely aware of the way it pulsed around her body. Here to her temple. There to her wrist. And there. *There.*

Her cheeks burned uncomfortably. Somehow *he* had

done this to her—brought to life in her something unknown and unwanted, with his silky taunts and that lazy way he had of looking at her. And he was so damned *blatant* about it, too!

Had she perhaps imagined that he would feel almost shy in her company, the way men so often did? Dazzled and slightly bemused by the impact of her looks and the status of her job? Especially someone who drove cars for a living, no matter how blessed he had been in the looks and body department.

She held her hands up to her hot cheeks, angry with herself for a physical reaction which seemed to be beyond her control. So it was time to take control. The important thing to remember was that if she *didn't* react to him then he wouldn't behave so provocatively. If she smiled serenely at his attempts to get under her skin then he would soon grow bored and stop it.

She found a battered-looking saucepan in one of the cupboards, and broke a fingernail into the bargain, and she was fractious and flustered by the time she returned, carrying two steaming mugs of black tea. But at least he had managed to get the fire going properly, and tentative flames were licking at one of the logs, bathing the room in soft, comforting shades of scarlet and orange.

She took her coat off and crept towards the fire's warmth. She handed him a mug, then crouched down on the floor, wishing she were wearing something warmer and more practical than a leather skirt and wondering why on earth she had, on such a cold day. Because it's fashionable, she reminded herself, and because the designer begged you to take it as a gift.

Jay Linur had removed his rather battered flying jacket too, but, unlike her, he had obviously made no concessions to sartorial elegance. His outfit was tough and practical. Faded jeans hugged his long, lean legs and he wore a warm dark sweater which softly clung to his torso. Firelight danced flames across the ruffled black hair, which was thick and slightly too long—giving him a buccaneer air which seemed to blend in well with the ancient fireplace.

He looked, she realised, completely at home as he lounged rather indolently along the rug, watching the progress of the fire—all rugged and arrogant confidence as he gazed into the flames, his thick lashes hooding his eyes. He turned his head to study her with lazy interest.

Keri put her mug down and winced as the ragged nail scratched against the palm of her hand.

'Hurt yourself?' he questioned softly.

'Not really, but I've broken my nail—and I can't even file it down—I left my make-up bag in the car!'

He gave a short laugh. 'Outside it's sub-zero, the snow is still coming down with no sign of a let-up, we're stranded God knows where, and all you can worry about is your damned fingernail!'

Keri was stung into defence. 'It isn't just vanity, if that's what you're implying—my job happens to depend on the state of my hands, among other things, and I was supposed to be doing a magazine-shoot for nail varnish next week!' It was, she realised, the first time in her life that she had ever felt the need to justify her job to anyone. So why—especially now, and to him of all people?

Jay took a mug of tea, sipped it and grimaced, wondering what type of world it was where a broken fingernail could mean anything at all other than just that. Not a world he could ever inhabit, that was for sure. Different strokes for different folks, he supposed.

He put the drink down in disgust. 'What the hell did you put in this? Arsenic?'

'Oh, please don't tempt me! I just used what was available,' she said crossly. 'Which were teabags which looked like they belonged in the Dark Ages!'

'Don't believe they had teabags in the Dark Ages,' he responded drily.

Keri almost laughed. Almost. Boundaries, she reminded herself. 'Do you have an answer for everything, Mr Linur?'

He looked at her. *Oh, yes.* The answer was staring him right in the face right now. Her lips were parted, so soft and so gleaming that they were practically begging to be kissed. He didn't have to approve of an icy beauty whose whole livelihood depended on the random paintbox of looks which nature had thrown together, but it didn't stop him wanting her.

'Try me,' he murmured. 'Ask me any question you like.'

There it was again—that tingy feeling, that sense of being out of control, as if she had drunk too much champagne too quickly. Keri swallowed. 'Okay. How's this for starters—just how are you proposing to get us out of here?'

CHAPTER THREE

JAY shrugged. 'I'm not,' he said flatly.

Keri raised her eyebrows. 'You mean that we're going to have to stay here for ever?'

He smiled at her sarcasm. Don't worry, sweetheart, he thought acidly—the idea appalls me just as much as it clearly does you. 'It's an intriguing prospect, but no. There's not a lot we can do, at least until the snow stops. Until then we'll just have to sit it out.'

The thought of that was making her more than uneasy. 'For how long?'

'Who knows? Until the thaw starts, or until someone finds us.'

And who knew how long that would be? 'You haven't even tried telephoning for help!' she accused.

'That's because there isn't a phone. I checked.'

'How can a place not have a telephone in this day and age?'

He shrugged his broad shoulders. It sounded like bliss to him. 'For the same reason that there's no television.' He shifted his legs slightly. 'I suspect that this is a holiday home and that the people who own it have deliberately decided to do away with all modern comforts.'

'Why would they do something like that?'

'The usual reasons. Televisions and telephones create stress, and some people don't like that stress. It's why they sail. Or climb mountains. Why they buy places like this—to escape.'

His voice had taken on a hard note, the tone of someone who was familiar with the word 'escape', and suddenly Keri longed for the safe and predictable. The sanctuary of her London flat—a clean and modernistic haven, as far removed from this big barn of a place as it was possible to imagine. Where heating was instantly produced by the touch of a button and cars and taxis moved comfortingly outside.

A world where men wore linen and silk and paid you clever compliments—not criticising you and then eyeing you with a kind of lazy watchfulness which had the ability to make you feel as flustered as a gauche young girl, and moving their legs as if to draw attention to their hard, muscular definition.

Quickly, she looked into the fire instead. 'Ironic, really,' she said, and thought how loud her voice sounded in the big, echoing room. 'A house designed for people to escape to, and we can't get out of it!'

'It could be a lot worse,' he said grimly. 'At least we're inside.'

Yes, they were. Alone. And Keri had been right—there were no rules in situation like this; they had to make them up as they went along. 'So what are we going to do?'

He sat up. 'Well, first we need to eat.'

'Eat?' she echoed blankly.

'You *do* eat, I suppose?' He watched her in the firelight. She was all bones, he thought—angles and shadows and long, slender legs, like a highly strung racehorse. The leather skirt clung to hips which were as narrow as a boy's, and although she did have breasts, they were tiny, like a young girl's. Jay liked his women curvy, with firm flesh that you could mould beneath the palms of your hands and soft hips that you could hold onto as you drove into them and catapulted them to pleasure. 'Though not a lot, by the look of you.'

'Oddly enough, the well-fed look isn't in vogue at the moment,' she said drily.

'I've never really understood why.'

'Because clothes look better on slender figures and that's a fact.'

Jay gave a half-smile. 'But nakedness looks better on a curvy figure, and *that's* a fact!'

'Well, thanks for bringing the conversation down-market!'

He shrugged. She thought that nakedness was down-market? 'That wasn't my intention.'

'You're saying you don't like thin women?'

His eyes narrowed. 'Careful, Keri,' he said softly. 'That sounds awfully like you're fishing for a compliment, and I'd guess you get more than the average quota of those.'

Yes, she did. It was part of the whole package which came with the way she looked. Men liked to look at her and to be seen with her—from her teen years she had been familiar with the phrase 'trophy girlfriend'. Yet beauty could be a double-edged sword. She had learned that, too. She earned her living through capitalising on her looks, then sometimes found herself wishing that people would see through to the person beneath—a person with all the insecurities of the next woman.

Defensively, she raked her hand back through her hair. 'Not a lot of danger of that at the moment, I imagine. I must look like I've been dragged through several hedges backwards.'

Her hair had been rumpled by the beanie and she hadn't brushed it, so it fell in ebony disarray over the pale silky sweater she wore. Her pale cheeks were tinged with roses, a combination of heat from the fire and the exertion of her walk through the snow. Yet she looked far more touchable and desirable than the ice princess in the diamonds and silver gown, who had pouted and swirled for the camera earlier.

'If you must know, you look a little...wild,' he said softly. 'Like a wood nymph who has just been woken out of a long sleep.'

Keri had never in her life been called 'wild', neither had she been compared to a wood nymph, and the poetic imagery of his words was so seductively powerful that for a moment she felt a slow, pulsing glow of pleasure. Until she reminded herself that this was madness.

Complete and utter madness.

Models had notoriously fragile egos—inevitable in a job in which you were judged so critically on physical attributes alone—but surely hers wasn't so bad that she needed praise from a house-breaking driver with a dark and dangerous air about him?

Suddenly she felt like a baby fish, swimming around in uncharted waters. 'Didn't you say something about food?'

'Sure.' He rose to his feet and wondered if she knew how cute she looked when she lost the frost princess look and let her lips soften like that. 'How about a fair division of labour? I'll go and see if I can find more fuel for the fire, and you can fix us a meal.'

'You'll be lucky!'

'Oh?'

'It's just that I don't cook. Can't cook,' she amended hurriedly as she saw him frown.

'I'm not expecting you to spit-roast a pig to impress me,' he bit back. 'Just rustle up any old thing.'

Impress him? *In your dreams.* 'There wasn't,' said Keri deliberately, 'anything much in the way of food, save for a few old tins.'

'Then get opening,' said Jay, and threw another log on the fire.

But Keri quickly discovered that this was easier said than done, because the tin-opener looked as though it should have been in a museum.

Jay walked out into the kitchen to find her slamming a tin frustratedly onto the table. Great, he thought! Have a tantrum, why don't you?

'Having problems?' he questioned laconically.

'*You* try using it!'

He picked up the tin and read the label. His voice was cool. 'Tinned peaches?'

'Well, obviously there's no *fresh* fruit—'

'That wasn't,' he exploded, 'what I meant!'

'Well, there was nothing much else to choose from.'

'If you think I'm existing on *tinned peaches*, then you are very much mistaken!'

'Well, would you mind opening them for *me*?'

He dealt with the can quickly, and thrust it away as if it had been contaminated, then bent to examine the contents of the cupboard, rummaging around until he produced a sealed pack of dried spaghetti and a solitary tin of meat sauce, which he slammed down onto the worktop. 'What's wrong with these?'

She suspected that it was going to be a mistake to try to explain her dietary requirements, but she forged ahead anyway. 'I don't eat wheat,' she said.

Jay shuddered. Bloody women and their food fads! Well, I *do*,' he said coolly. 'So would you mind heating these up?' He saw her open her mouth to protest. 'Unless you'd rather tend to the fire?'

She could see the mocking look of challenge in his eyes, as if he knew perfectly well that she had never 'tended' a fire in her life. Lots of people she knew hadn't—so why was he trying to make her feel as though she was in some way inadequate? Just because he was the original cave-dweller, that didn't mean the rest of the world had to follow suit. Very well, she would heat his revolting food for him. 'I'll cook.'

'Good.' And he turned and walked out of the kitchen without another word, thinking that she was undeniably beautiful but about as much use as an igloo in a heatwave. He cast an assessing eye over the fuel. There were a couple of cupboards he'd noticed upstairs; they might yield an armful of blankets which they would need to see the night through. The strain of spending a night closeted with her made a tiny muscle work at the side of his temple, and then he remembered the only room they hadn't explored. Maybe the cellar might come up trumps. Something to ease the tension.

When he returned to the kitchen it was with a look of triumph on his face and a bottle of dusty wine in his hand. He put it carefully on the table.

'Look at that! Would you believe it?'

Fractiously, Keri looked up from the steaming pot. Half the spaghetti had snapped on the way into it, and she had scalded her finger into the bargain. 'It's a bottle of wine—so what?'

'It is not any old bottle of wine,' he contradicted, running his thumb reverentially over the label, as if he was carressing a woman's skin. 'It just happens to be a bottle of St Julien du Beau Caillou.'

His voice had deepened with appreciation and his French accent was close to perfect. Keri couldn't have been more amazed if he had suddenly leapt up onto the table and started tap dancing.

'You know about wine, do you?'

Jay's eyes glittered. The tone of her question said it all. 'Surprising for a common-or-garden driver, is that what you mean?' he drawled. 'Thought I'd be a beer man, did you?'

'I hadn't given it much thought, actually.'

Liar, he thought. You'd placed me in the little box of your sterotypical expectations. Though, when he stopped to think about it, hadn't he done exactly the same to her? Except that she seemed to be living up to hers—with her faddy eating habits and general inability to cope with the practicalities which misfortune sometimes threw up at you. In fact, she seemed pretty good at looking beautiful and not a lot else, as far as he could make out.

He found a corkscrew and raised his dark eyebrows at her in question.

'So, will you be joining me, Keri?' he queried. 'Or holding out for a glass of water?'

She *would* normally have had water, yes—damn him—but tonight Keri had never felt more in need of a drink in her life. And at least it might make the time go a little faster. Might even calm her frayed nerves and help her to sleep. She gave the pot another stir. She didn't even want to *think* about the sleeping arrangements.

'Yes, I'll join you in a glass,' she said repressively.

'How very gracious of you,' he murmured. He eased the cork from the bottle with a satisfying pop and, as always, the sensual significance of that didn't escape him.

Keri looked down at the saucepan and grimaced. She had seen more appetising things served up in a dogbowl. 'Shall I dish this out?'

Hunting through a cupboard for glasses, Jay glanced over his shoulder. 'Can't wait,' he murmured.

He poured two glasses of wine and watched while she picked up the heavy saucepan with two hands and carried it over to the sink. Hell, her wrists were so thin they looked as if they might snap.

'I can't find a colander anywhere.'

'Give it to me,' he said tersely. He rolled the sleeves of his sweater up and took it from her before she could drop it, using the lid to drain it, shaking his dark head a little as he did so. 'I can't believe that you've got to…what age are you?'

She supposed it would be pointless to tell him that it was none of his business. 'Twenty-six.'

'Twenty-*six*!' He carried back the pot. 'And you can't even cope with spaghetti!'

'This is the twenty-first century!' she retorted. 'And it isn't written into the female contract that she needs to cook!'

'Then pity the poor man you marry,' he offered.

'Well, there's no need to worry on that score,' she answered, more testily than she had intended, because her attention had been caught by the sight of his arms—all tanned and muscular and sprinkled with hair as dark as his head. At his wrist was a slim plait of leather.

A stir of interest quickened his blood. 'You mean there's no likely candidate on the horizon?'

She heard the sultry change in his voice and her eyes met his in a long, unspoken moment across the table. Its impact was such that she felt as if he had turned her to stone. Or clay. Yes, clay—far more malleable than stone, and that was exactly what she felt like at that moment. Clay—all damp and squidgy. Malleable.

Keri was used to a man looking at her with interest—she had encountered it often enough in the past— but never, never with such devastating *effect*. The slanting eyes glittered only momentarily, and the hard smile was so brief it might almost have been an illusion, but it was enough.

Enough to what? To set her pulses racing with the

knowledge that this was a man quite unlike any other she had ever come into contact with. Steely-edged and strong and capable—and yet, inexplicably, one who could read a wine label in the most perfect accent.

She wanted to say *Don't look at me that way!* She wanted to tell him that he didn't have a hope in hell if *that* was what he was thinking—even while a Keri she didn't know or recognise was wondering what it would be liked to be imprisoned in the embrace of a man with arms as muscular and as powerful as his.

'Keri?' he said softly.

His voice seemed to come from a great distance away, and her own, in response, sounded low, husky—a world away from her usual cool tones. 'Y-yes?'

'Get a couple of plates down, would you?'

He saw the flustered look in her eyes as she quickly turned away. So she had felt it too—that indefinable chemistry which existed between the sexes and sometimes shimmered through the air when you were least expecting it.

No, that wasn't quite true. *He* had been expecting it. He was as hot-blooded as the next man. Mix up an attractive man and an attractive woman, stir in a little bit of circumstance, and usually the result would be fairly predictable. Jay had been used to women coming on to him since he was old enough to want them to.

But Miss Beauty was different. This was a woman who would put up defences—probably a necessity when you looked the way she did. She would be wary and on her guard against men who wanted her—and what man in his right mind wouldn't?

And you didn't get a woman like that to want you back—not unless you played her very carefully.

Keri put a plate down on the table with a hand which wasn't quite steady.

'You aren't eating?' he asked.

'I'm not eating that,' she said. 'I'll have the peaches.'

'You're kidding?'

'No, Jay, I am not. They will do just fine—and you should never eat a heavy meal before—I mean...after six,' she finished, licking at lips which were suddenly parched. She had been about to say *before bedtime*, but she'd bitten the words back in time.

'Suit yourself.' He shrugged his shoulders and began to ladle the food out, liking the way she'd said his name—real slow and sweet, as if she'd dipped the single syllable in honey.

She watched as he heaped on what seemed to be an enormous amount of food.

'You honestly aren't planning to eat all that yourself?'

He flicked her a glance. 'I have a big appetite,' he said gravely.

Keri felt her knees grow weak. This was awful. Or was it inevitable that once sensual awareness had shivered into the mind it was impossible to think straight, or to forget it? He's your *driver*, Keri, she reminded herself. 'Then you should be careful,' she said coolly as she dolloped peaches into a dish. 'Or one day that muscle will turn to fat.'

'I don't think so. If a man stays active he doesn't get fat, and I am *very* active.' He smiled. 'Now, let's take all these goodies next door. We can sit in front of the roaring fire and then…'

'Then what?' she questioned, her voice rising in alarm.

'Then you can tell me the story of your life.' His eyes gleamed with anticipation. 'So far.'

CHAPTER FOUR

SOMEWHERE between the kitchen and the cavernous sitting room Keri gave herself the kind of silent pep-talk that she hadn't really needed since she was in that hormonal state of mid-teen flux which made girls think their heads were composed of cotton wool.

There was no denying that he was a gorgeous man, nor that she seemed to be attracted to him, in a rather confusing, pulse-racing kind of way. But that was hardly surprising. You would need to have been made out of stone not to acknowledge his physical presence or his to-die-for face. And he had taken charge and got them here safely, and there was an unmistakable appeal about that too. A man who could protect definitely did appeal to an age-old and very feminine need which until this moment she hadn't realised she possessed.

Yet it was more than that. All her adult life she had mixed with men who were good-looking, who probably could match him muscle for muscle—though theirs was of the type which was honed at the gym, which she suspected Jay Linur's wasn't. He looked as if he had been born strong and capable.

But looks were just the exterior package—she of all people knew what they could hide—and the thing about Jay Linur which seemed to set him apart was a kind of inner confidence and ease. And, yes, it was surprising for a driver, and particularly surprising that he didn't seem to be fazed by the fact that he found himself in these isolated surroundings with a woman who would usually have the most confident man slightly lost for words.

Perhaps it was because he had nothing to lose that he seemed to have the ability to treat her as she was so rarely treated—as if she was just another woman and he was just another man.

Which was all he was. A man who was capable in crisis, but ultimately a man she would never see again once that crisis was resolved. So she had better forget all about the hard, rugged profile and stop snatching surreptitious little looks at the hard-packed body.

The fire was roaring now—a glorious blaze of amber and crimson logs sending off the most delicious smell as they burned—and she saw that he had put a small pile of blankets down to warm, well out of spitting range.

Keri sniffed the air, her heart hammering, trying to draw her attention away from the heap of blankets and its implications. Where on earth where they going to *sleep* tonight? With an effort, she dragged her thoughts back to the fragrant smoke. 'Mmm.'

'Applewood,' he informed her as he put the tray down. 'And there was dried lavender scattered in the bottom of the basket. Good, isn't it?'

Keri nodded. He had parked his long-legged frame on the floor, and after a moment's indecision she joined him. Because it made sense. This was where the warmth was—as close to the fire as possible.

But it seemed too intimate—a feeling not helped by

the fire, nor by the fact that the candlelight created a romantic look to the room. Never before had she realised the seductive potential of candlelight even though she had sat in countless restaurants which used it. She told herself that the soft, flickering light was designed to create a romantic 'mood', and she must be sure and remember that the mood they were creating here was an illusion.

He poured her a glass of wine. When she was pensive like that she looked ridiculously young—softer and sweeter. But models were tough—they had to be. He'd known a few in his time—women who wore so many different masks that in the end you wondered whether there was any real substance beneath.

'Here,' he said.

'Thanks.' She turned her head to take it from him, startled by the cold, searching light in his eyes, as if he was examining her under a microscope, as a scientist would.

'Eat,' he said sardonically. 'Mmm—those peaches look so tempting!'

Keri had trained her appetite rigorously over the years. She had learnt to regard hunger as a normal state; you needed to if you were to fit into the clothes you were expected to wear on shoots or on the catwalk. Unlike most of her peers, she didn't smoke any more—and whenever she wanted more food than she knew was necessary to maintain her slender frame she usually went for a walk, or read a book, or arranged flowers. Displacement therapy—none of which were remotely possible here and now.

She ate a peach and took a large gulp of wine, trying

to ignore the smell of Jay's food wafting towards her and trying not to watch as he curled the spaghetti round his fork and ate it with a pleasure which was almost sensual. How could some meaty slush like that smell so…so tempting?

For a while he said nothing, just ate with slow and obvious enjoyment. Then he moved a forkful towards her. 'Here. Have some,' he coaxed softly.

The smell was tantalising. 'I don't eat wheat,' she said weakly. 'Remember? Or…or red meat… particularly out of a tin.' She screwed her nose up in an expression of disgust she didn't quite feel.

'Suit yourself.' He transferred the forkful back and ate it himself, and began to scoop up another.

On the one hand she knew exactly what he was doing—trying to tempt her into eating when he knew she didn't want to—and yet there was this unrecognisable Keri who didn't care, whose stomach was empty and rumbling.

'Go on,' he said. 'You know you want to.'

His eyes were brilliant, hard and gleaming like a diamond, and now another loaded fork was just inches away from her mouth. Keri responded instinctively, her mouth opening like a goldfish, and he ladled the food in before she had had time for second thoughts.

She closed her eyes and ate it, afraid to see the mocking look of triumph in his, but sheer greed—a new and rather frightening animal—took over and she gave an instinctive little moan of pleasure.

'Like it?' he murmured.

Her eyes snapped open, but it was not triumph she read in his eyes, but relish, as if he was pleased to see her discovering the delight of indulging her hunger and then satisfying it.

Keri shrugged and gave him a rueful look. 'It's delicious.'

He put some more on the fork and held it up to her. 'See what you've been missing?'

She shook her head. 'No, honestly, I couldn't...'

'Shut up,' he said, but gently. 'And eat.'

The second forkful went the way of the first, and two more followed. She shook her head. 'I mustn't have any more—really, Jay—I'm eating all your supper!'

He considered telling her that he had deliberately put enough food on the plate for two, but decided against it. If she thought it had been pre-planned then her defences might go up, and that he most definitely didn't want.

The heaped fork moved from where it hovered close to her mouth back to his, and his lips closed round it. Something about that gesture was deeply erotic. There was silence, save for the spitting of the fire, and her eyes were fixed to his, as if they had drawn her in by their sheer, mesmeric power, rendering her incapable of breaking the gaze.

He licked his lips and smiled. 'One for me, and one for...you.'

Keri opened her mouth like an obedient child, feeling both weak and strong as he fed her again. The food was filling her full of warmth and energy, but it was an odd, slumberous kind of energy, and with it came helplessness as she recognised that never before had she realised that eating in itself could be a very sexual act.

Very soon the plate was completely clean, and Jay surveyed it with satisfaction and then looked at her. 'What a pity it's all gone. I was enjoying that.' He meant the feeding, not the eating.

Another gulp of wine. 'Yes.'

He glanced down at the dish of peaches—all golden and glistening and slickly luscious—and the stealthy beat of desire grew even stronger. 'We've still got pudding,' he said softly, and his eyes gleamed out a silent challenge. 'Your turn now.'

But Keri couldn't. Just the thought of slipping the soft fruit into his mouth was enough to make her feel very churned up indeed. Her hand would shake—she just knew it would—and then he might get some inkling of what was going on inside her head.

And her body.

Her limbs felt weighted and deliciously lethargic, and yet there was the sensation of blood beating like thick syrup through her veins, of her fingers and toes inexorably unfurling, along with her senses.

She shook her head, grounded and yet unbearably dizzy. 'Not for me, thanks, I'm full—but help yourself.'

Jay didn't want the peaches, not unless she was going to feed them to him the way he had done to her, but his brief feeling of disappointment was replaced by an infinitely better one of expectation. He thought of the blonde who had been pursuing him these past months—she wouldn't have fed him the peaches either, but by now she probably would have had half his clothes off and be busy feeding herself on his body.

It had been a long time, he realised, since he had wanted something he wasn't sure he was going to get.

'I'll pass too,' he said idly, and leaned back against the sofa instead, cradling the claret in his hand and watching the living beauty of the fire. 'So, how long have you been a model?'

The question broke the mood she had longed to be broken, but Keri had to fight her unreasonable sense of dismay. Conversation like this was safer by far— and surely that was preferable?

The wine had made her garrulous. 'Since I left school—well, actually, that's not quite true—I was still *at* school.' She thought how at ease he looked, lying there, one leg bent at the knee as he balanced his weight negligently on his elbow, the wine sending out dappled ruby reflections over his strong fingers, and she found herself imagining those fingers running with instinctive mastery over her body. Oh, for heaven's *sake*, Keri, she chided herself—since when did you start having fantasies like that?

'Mmm?' He raised his dark eyebrows, as if to prompt her, trying to rid himself of the image of her in pigtails and a school uniform.

With an effort she dragged her mind back to the subject in question. 'I was visiting London with my sister—'

'Is she a model too?'

Keri shook her head. 'No, she's a mother.' And a widow. She rushed on, the thoughts of that too painful. 'We were just having a coffee at Waterloo Station when a woman came over and asked if I'd ever thought about modelling.'

'The way it happens in all the movies?'

'Sort of.'

'And had you thought about it before that?'

Keri shrugged. 'It had crossed my mind from time to time—other people were always telling me I should try—but...'

His eyes gleamed. 'But?'

'Well, what I really wanted to do was interior design. Added to that I was very tall and very skinny, and that makes you kind of self-conscious.'

'Not the best quality for someone hoping for a career in front of the cameras, I would have thought,' he observed thoughtfully.

She had thought that too, but had soon discovered that a skinny and insecure girl who towered over her peers could become someone else in front of the camera. When it was make-believe it was easy to pretend that you were supremely confident and at ease with yourself.

'I was lucky,' she said truthfully. 'All that self-consciousness just vanished in front of the lens—and my face is one of those which looks better in photographs than it does in real life.'

He didn't agree. He thought she looked softer and more touchable in real life—far more of a woman when she wasn't acting up for the lens. 'The camera loves you, you mean?'

She nodded. 'So far—touch wood.'

'And what happens when it no longer does?'

Keri frowned. With uncanny precision he had

alighted on every model's most abiding fear—of being last-year's face, the face the public have tired of. 'Some people go on for years,' she said defensively.

'That isn't what I asked,' he mused. 'I was asking *when*—because presumably few continue into old age?'

Keri sipped at her wine again, because that seemed easier than answering straight away. He really did seem uncomfortably good at asking the right sort of questions. Or the wrong. She couldn't think of an answer that would satisfy him—or herself. That occasionally she dreamed of a 'normal' life? If she said she wanted to get married and start a family it would sound needy, as if she was unfulfilled because she didn't have a man.

And that wasn't true—she couldn't even lose herself in the everywoman fantasy about one day falling in love with a man who matched her every emotional and physical need. The two seemed intertwined; you couldn't have one without the other—and when you had never had one in particular...

She was aware that he was still looking at her questioningly, and she hoped that those discerning eyes hadn't noticed the fact that her cheeks had grown warm—but even if they had she guessed she could always blame it on the fire.

She stared into the flickering flames. 'I've never really given much thought to the future.'

'So the interior design went by the wayside?'

'I guess it did.' She looked up at him and met the question in his eyes with a shrug. 'I've done a few projects—just for fun, really—my own apartment and my sister's house, and I loved doing those.'

'So why not switch careers?'

'Because I haven't quite reached the stage of ageing has-been,' she remarked sardonically. 'And even if I wanted to it's notoriously difficult to break into something like that unless you have experience, and to gain experience you have to start at the bottom of the ladder.' She gave a grimace. 'And I'm not sure I'd want to do that. Not now.'

'You could always branch out on your own,' he suggested.

Keri frowned. Since when had *he* become an expert on careers? He was hardly in a position to offer advice! She switched the interrogation from him to her. 'And what about you? I mean, do you plan to be a driver for the rest of your life?'

Her subtle emphasis on the word *driver* didn't escape him, and Jay smiled as he refilled their glasses. She wanted to put some distance between them, to tell him that he was stepping out of line by asking such searching questions, particularly given his lowly status.

He sighed. People got so hung up on status—they let it blind them to the things that really mattered and they hid behind it, as if it could protect them from the world.

'Well, that's the beauty of a job like this,' he said expansively. 'Easy come, easy go.'

How casual he made it sound—and yet it was interesting, in a funny kind of way. She never mixed with men who didn't put ambition at the top of their list of desires. 'And have you always done it?' she asked curiously. 'Driving, I mean?'

Jay almost laughed aloud, and if he hadn't been so easy in his own skin he might have taken offence at her assumption. Did she *really* think that he would have been happy sitting behind the wheel of a car all these years, ferrying around people like her, who were so far removed from the real world as to be on another planet?

His expansive mood evaporated. He threw another log on the fire. He didn't broadcast his past; people—especially women—seemed to be fascinated to the point of intrusion by a life which had been composed largely of excitement and danger and deprivation and discipline. His mouth tightened.

'Not always, no.'

His evasion interested her too, because in her experience men were renowned for wanting to talk about themselves.

'Oh? What kind of things have you done?'

Now she was very definitely patronising him, and it had the effect of making him want to master and subdue her. He suppressed it. For the moment.

'I was in the US Navy,' he said shortly. 'A SEAL.'

Keri screwed her nose up, but he didn't appear to be joking. 'What's that, exactly? I mean, I've heard of Navy SEALs, but I don't know much about them.'

He relaxed a little. She didn't know much about them. This was one of the reasons he'd chosen to come back to England—over here there was none of the SEAL-as-hero stuff which he'd lived with since the age of eighteen.

'What is a SEAL?' He played it down, the way he always did. 'Well, we root and toot and parachute,' he murmured, his eyes glittering as he saw her look of utter incomprehension. 'We're a combination of frogman and paratrooper,' he explained. 'We blow things up, dive to the deepest depths and jump from insane heights.' *And we always get the pretty girl.*

'So, were you an officer?'

This time Jay did laugh. He guessed that type of differentiation would be *very* important to her. One of the ratings certainly wouldn't be good enough for Miss Beauty. 'Yes, Keri,' he answered gravely. 'I was an officer.'

That explained a lot. The strength, the resourcefulness, the cool confidence in a crisis. And the body, of course—hard, honed muscle like that was the result of years of training. She had been right—you didn't get to look like that if you just frequented the gym, no matter how often.

And the US bit explained the slight drawl, the accent she had never heard before—and it might also explain the ease with which he spoke to her, because weren't Americans better at breaking down class barriers than their English counterparts?

'So you *are* American?'

Her body language was relaxing into the conversation, her long, long legs as coltish as they'd looked in his driver's mirror. Jay remembered the brief, tantalising view of her lacy stocking-tops and he felt the deep beat of his pulse in response. Maybe he would talk all she liked, if that was what it took to loosen her up.

'Half and half,' he said. 'Or maybe neither. That happens sometimes when you're torn between two cultures.' He saw her interested, inquisitive gaze. In any other situation he would have changed the subject—moved it on or away—but this was not any other situation, it was this one, and its very isolation seemed designed to draw out confidences he would usually have kept locked away.

'I grew up in both countries after my parents divorced,' he said tightly. 'My father was American and my mother British—but I hold dual nationality and that's what qualified me to join.' Along with an endurance test designed purposely to weed out all but the very toughest of the tough.

Keri blinked in confusion. Surely being in the US Navy was a lot more preferable to *this*? 'And did you er, did you *have* to leave?'

'You mean, was I kicked out?'

'No, I didn't mean that—'

'Oh, yes, you did, and no, I wasn't—it was just time to leave.'

'You'd had enough?'

Yes, he'd had enough. Too many demonstrations of how ultimately frail man could be—too many reminders of the shortness of life and the inevitability of death. It was a young man's game—always had been and always would be—and it needed a young man's vigour and invincible belief in himself. Once that was gone you were no good to anyone—least of all yourself. Or to people who needed you...

'Something like that,' he said shortly, and this time he could do nothing to stop the memories which came back to haunt him—nothing like as powerful as they had been in those early days and nights, but still powerful enough to make him flinch. Memories of death and betrayal which were light-years away from most men's experiences. And honour. Always honour. Honour and service.

'That kind of job has its own limited life-span—a bit like yours, probably.'

A muscle was working in the strong face, and for the first time Keri noticed a tiny, tiny scar which tracked down it. She reached her hand out, as if to touch it, but she did not. 'How did you do that?'

His eyes grew cold and hard, like flint.

'Oh, just something,' he said dismissively.

Keri knew when not to probe any further, and she dragged her attention away from his face, feeling curiously disorientated. She was alone in a deserted place with a man she scarcely knew—a man with muscles which looked real and a scarred face. A real man, not a silk-clad concoction of the city.

She should be scared and on her guard, but she wasn't. Inside, she felt warm and replete from the unexpectedly delicious food, and lulled by the velvet glow of the rich wine. She stretched her legs out, as if testing how far they would reach, feeling at peace, something beyond her control subduing the knowledge that this was somehow *wrong*—how could it be?

All she was doing was making the best of a bad situation. Only she was fast coming to the conclusion that it wasn't so bad at all. Quite the contrary. The fact that he had been in the Navy gave him a life other than as a driver, and somehow it made her feel *safe*.

She felt her gaze drawn towards him again and found that his attention was on her. It was a curious yet assessing look, and maybe she should have looked away, but she didn't—didn't want to. His eyes were dark and glittering—she still couldn't make out what colour they were—and all she was aware of was that a ripple of awareness had begun to lick at her skin.

There was a sudden soft hush in the air. Jay saw her relax. Saw the reflex as her fingers lost the tension which had stiffened them, like the way a woman relaxed after orgasm, and he felt the irresistible kick of desire as he put his empty wine glass down in the grate.

There were times to move and times to stay, and he would have wagered every cent he had that she wanted him to move. And why not? They had a long night to get through.

Flopping into her dark eyes was her over-long fringe, and he reached out and touched it, as if to brush it away. But he didn't. The feel of her skin was so soft that he left the tip of his finger right there, began to curl one of the wayward strands around it.

It felt curiously and inexplicably right. She should have shaken her head away, or demanded to know just what he thought he was playing at. And what did she do? She said one little word.

'Jay...' The word came out as a murmured and breathy little sound; it didn't sound a bit like her.

'Mmm?' He heard the catch in her voice and felt the race of his heart. 'Don't you like me tidying up your hair for you, Keri? It's all mussed.'

But he wasn't tidying up her hair at all, she thought

wildly. The hair lay neglected as instead he stroked his fingertips down her face to the line of her jaw, and she shivered beneath what was outwardly such an innocent gesture but which felt like the most erotic thing she had ever felt before. And how ridiculous was that?

'Don't you?' he urged.

'It's okay,' she admitted.

'Only okay?' he purred. 'Then I must be losing my touch.'

The arrogant boast should have raised her defences, for it implied that he was a consummate expert where touching women was concerned, but all Keri felt was a debilitating curiosity to know whether he was.

Losing his touch? Like hell he was! Helplessly, her eyes fluttered to a close as he began to stroke her neck. She lifted her head so that more of it was available to him, and the ripple of sensation became a stronger swell which pulled her along with it.

Keri felt pure excitement and expectancy as his touch danced sweet, tantalising pathways over her skin, as if he was opening up sensitive nerve-endings for the first time. How could the simple brush of someone's fingers against someone else's neck be so…so *electric*?

'Sh-should we be doing this?' she questioned unsteadily.

CHAPTER FIVE

JAY nearly said that they weren't doing anything...not yet, but instead he smiled a brief smile. 'It isn't a capital crime, is it, sweetheart, for me to touch you?'

'That...that wasn't quite what I meant.'

'Oh, I get you.' The smile hardened into one of granite. 'You mean...that it's unprofessional?' he queried acidly. 'Because I'm just the driver and you're the...client?'

Her eyes flew open at the use of a word which was open to rampant misunderstanding, but he shushed her with a shake of his dark head and his smile became cajoling.

'But I'm not working now, Keri,' he said. 'Neither are you. And what we do in our own time is nobody's business but our own. Is it?'

Put that way, it seemed to make sense. 'No,' she agreed slowly. 'I guess not.' She couldn't think straight; she was lulled by his touch, by the blinding light in his eyes and the sensation of her blood growing thick and heated in her veins, wanting him to touch her some more. Somewhere that wasn't her neck.

'Such a beautiful neck,' he mused, his voice deepening like a connoisseur. 'Like a swan—so pale and pure—such beautiful lines.'

'Why, thank you,' she murmured, once again taken

aback by the elegance of his words, which seemed so at odds with his tough, no-nonsense exterior.

She smiled, and Jay smiled back, knowing what a woman wanted when she smiled at you like that. She was so accessible, so unexpectedly compliant, and he leaned forward and placed his mouth where before there had been only his fingers, opening his lips slightly as they touched against her neck, so that he breathed soft and warm against the silk of her skin. He felt her instinctive shivering response beneath him, and the biting of her fingernails into his shoulders as she reached up her hands to grip him.

'Oh!' she breathed.

He continued to graze his lips against her neck, sensing that she wanted him to kiss her properly, but he knew from experience that the best way to turn a woman on was to make her wait. The slow, slow burn. But he felt her distracted little movement, the restless shake of her head, and suddenly it wasn't so easy to do that.

He lifted his lips from her neck and took her face between the palms of his hands, giving her one hard look before he lowered his mouth to hers. He kissed her long and deep, and it was as if someone had just pressed a button marked 'sizzle'.

Her lips opened hungrily, greedily to his, and she swayed against him, making no protest when he pulled her to the floor and into his arms, and through the desire which was fast building in his groin he felt momentarily taken aback.

He had expected ice, not fire. He had expected to have to work a lot harder than this... His fingers moved experimentally to her thigh, waiting for her to sit up and tell him that this was outrageous, but she did no such thing, just made a little moan of encouragement. He smiled as his fingertips roved upwards, to find the lacy provocation of her stocking-top and the silky skin above it. So his first impression had been the wrong one; she was obviously a lot more physical than he had thought.

She wriggled with pleasure as she felt the splay of his fingers over her inner thigh. 'Jay!' she whispered.

'Mmm?' His mouth was on her breast now, suckling at her tiny breasts through the thin sweater she wore, and her fingers moved distractedly to thread themselves in his hair. That was when he moved over her and began to kiss her.

'Oh, God—Jay!' she moaned.

He raised his head and looked down at her, his eyes glittering and impenetrable as his fingers tiptoed over her cool yet heated flesh. 'What is it?' he questioned unsteadily.

'That's good,' she breathed, a note of wonder in her voice. 'So good.'

'Tell me about it,' he said, in an odd strained voice, as his hand moved further and alighted on the delicious moistness of her panties. She writhed and mouthed a husky little plea until he lowered his head and began to kiss her again, feeling like a man who had tried to light a match and then discovered he had dynamite in his hands.

Maybe it was because it was so unexpected that the desire he felt was close to explosion point already, and

Jay sucked in a dry, painful breath. Take it easy, he told himself. And take it slow.

But she didn't seem to want that. He knew enough about women to realise that she was pretty close to the top. Roughly, he slid the leather skirt up her thighs and her legs parted for him. She was so warm and so wet. With a little groan he reached up and slithered the panties down, noting the way that she lifted her feet to help him. Oh, yes—she wanted this—maybe even more than he did.

He pushed the skirt still further up. Leather wasn't the easiest material in the world to cope with, but there wasn't a skirt invented which couldn't be slid up, and soon he had it rucked up round her hips, leaving her deliciously accessible. And that was when he discovered that she was shaved completely bare, and the unexpected novelty of *that* made him want to take her there and then, but he held back. He was good at holding back—a lifetime of discipline and training paid dividends at times like this.

'Oh, my,' he murmured, on a low, sweet note of anticipation. 'Now, what shall we do next?'

'Anything,' she gasped. 'Everything.'

She was so eager! 'How could any man resist an invitation like that?' he murmured.

Keri experienced a mixture of disbelief and satisfaction as he moved downwards and she felt the tickle of his dark hair between her knees. Her head fell back—she had never liked this, never let... And then his lips were brushing up her thigh, his tongue slicking its way up and up until it found the most intimate part of her, and then her mouth parted and she gave a tiny scream of pleasure.

It was as if someone had catapulted her into another dimension, or as if someone else had suddenly started inhabiting her skin. She began to move her head from side to side—and surely those gasping little cries weren't *hers*?

'Oh, Jay,' she moaned softly. 'Jay, Jay, *Jay*!'

Through a sensation so intense that she thought she might pass out, some tiny voice in her head reached out to tell her that she shouldn't be letting this happen, that someone had to stop it and it had to be her.

But she couldn't.

Wouldn't.

Not now.

Especially not now, because something was happening to her and she wanted it so badly that she felt she would die if she didn't get it. Something which was filling her with a fast-building heat and an unbearable hunger, and she was terrified in case it would go away and she would fail to reach it.

'Jay!' she whispered, on a tiny, pleading note.

He didn't answer. He was too busy orchestrating her response with the seasoned flick of his tongue—tasting the sweetness of her unmistakable woman's taste, teasing her with a featherlight touch which soon had her sobbing.

Keri heard her own wild, uninhibited cries, but they seemed to come from a distant place—and maybe she'd invented them, because she never cried out like that before. As if she was desperate and yearning and scared and seeking all at the same time—like being on a runaway train which just wouldn't stop.

He felt her tense, and knew she was close, and he licked at her luxuriously until he felt her spasm against his mouth. He held onto her hips while she bucked against him, tasting her sweet surrender. It seemed to go on and on and on, and he remembered reading somewhere that when women shaved like that it made them more sensitive. Was that why she had done it? To increase the power of her orgasm? Then he really *had* misjudged her.

Keri's breath shuddered to a slower pace while she alternated between the drenching bask of pleasure and the shaken sensation that this was what had eluded her all along. So this was why sex turned people's lives upside down and inside out and back again.

And it had taken a virtual stranger to show her.

A great bursting ache of pleasure seeped its warmth through her body, and as he came to lie over her again she breathed one heartfelt word.

'Beautiful.'

He smiled, and touched his lips to her nose. 'Yes, you are.'

'That wasn't what I meant.'

'I know it wasn't.' He brushed a strand of hair away from her damp cheek. 'Now, look at me.'

Cautiously, she opened her eyes, terrified of what she would find written in his. What would he think of her now? So wild and so free and with such little provocation? But there was no censure on his face, though the shadows thrown up by the firelight onto those cheekbones made him look faintly formidable. And his mouth was as soft as his eyes—if only she knew what colour they were—as if he were about to enjoy a delicious feast, and she felt strangely shy, the power of what had just happened to her making her realise just how inexperienced she really was. Especially compared to him. And now? What now? Could there be more, and as good as that? Suddenly her starved body was greedy.

He touched his lips to hers. She could taste herself on his mouth, and that felt so unbelievably intimate that she sighed, snaking her arms around his neck to pull him closer. She could feel the hard, flat planes of his body, and the cradle of him, where he was harder still.

'That's *good*,' he murmured approvingly. He ran his hand over the skirt, which was rucked up almost to her waist. 'Is it warm enough to take this off, do you think?'

The fire was blazing, and her skin was still glowing in the aftermath, but it seemed that his question had not really required an answer. He was pulling off his sweater with a practised hand and tossing it aside.

Underneath, a slim-fitting dark T-shirt moulded itself to the muscled sinews of his chest and he peeled that off too. She saw the rich, tawny skin, the sprinkling of hair which arrowed down to the waistband of his jeans. Oh, but he was magnificent! The way she had always known that a real man should look.

She trickled her fingertips over the oiled silk of his torso. And he felt the way that a real man should feel too. 'You are so beautiful,' she said shyly.

He smiled as he observed her rapt preoccupation

with his skin. For a moment there he had thought she was going to be a selfish lover—taking, never giving. Wanting only pleasure for herself without wanting to give any back. And thank heavens he had been wrong.

She was coming back to life, and the contrast between this near shyness and how wild she'd been earlier was making him feel as weak as water. Then he glanced down and saw the clean lines of her slim body, reminded himself that she was shaved—and how many women did *that*? So it figured that the shyness was probably just a show, to salve her conscience, to make her feel less guilty about what she had just let him do to her.

'Want to take my jeans off for me, Keri?' He ran her hand down the shaft of his thigh and glittered her a provocative look. 'I'm just putty in your hands.'

Insecurity threatened to swamp her as she felt like a complete novice in the light of his obvious and breathtaking experience. She dared not say no, but her hands were trembling so much that she was afraid she might make a complete mess of such a simple act.

He saw the shaking fingers and smiled. 'Don't hurt me now, will you?' he drawled mockingly.

'I...I'll do my best.'

Jay gave a low laugh—weren't the English the masters, or the mistresses in this case, of understated irony? She had just had the most mind-blowing orgasm and now she was fumbling around like a sweet young virgin.

Somehow she managed to get his jeans off, and everything else too, her heart beginning to thunder again when he was finally naked, lazily and assuredly naked, save for the narrow plaited band at his wrist. But she didn't have time for second thoughts, because he was skimming the rest of her clothes off until she, too, was naked. He pulled her against him, wrapping his long, strong limbs around her, the sensation of his warmth and his strength driving every thought from her mind other than the realisation that she wanted—no, *needed* him to make love to her. Properly.

'Oh, Jay.'

'What is it?'

How had this happened, and when? Her head fell heavily to his shoulder as he began to stroke at her breasts, and wherever he touched her it was though he burned into her, making her nerve endings shriek aloud in recognition. 'You make me feel...' The words trailed off, for there were no words for the way he made her feel.

'Wanton?' he prompted, his words molten whispers against her cheek. 'Because that's the way I want you to feel, Keri. And now just feel me. Go on, sweetheart—feel how much I want you.'

She touched him, feeling him spring against her, so hard and so virile, and it was as though she had never been intimately acquainted with a man's body before.

And maybe she hadn't. Not like this. Filled with a sudden need to explore him. As if she wanted to touch and kiss and caress every single centimetre of his body. She reached down to encircle him in her hand, curling her fingers around the rocky shaft, and some instinct made her writhe her hips against him even while she bent her head to tease and graze at his nipple with her teeth.

Jay shuddered beneath her touch. God, she was passionate! Too passionate, because suddenly he knew that he could not wait, that this was good, but not good enough. He had never felt so full, so hard, so ready to burst, and he wanted more. Everything. The real thing.

Decisively and irrevocably he moved over her, and Keri's eyes snapped open in alarm. 'You will...you will use something, won't you?'

It was a sensible question, and one which did not need to be asked, since his hand was already reaching out for the pocket of his jeans—yet it irritated the hell out of him and he wasn't sure why.

But he found what he was looking for and gave up thinking, sliding the condom on and then sliding straight into her. He groaned because she was so tight—oh, so beautifully tight—that it was almost over before it had begun, until he reined right back.

As he moved he lost himself in her heat, hearing her gasp in time with each exquisite thrust, and he heard some deep, primeval sound dragged from deep within his own lungs. Maybe it was because it had been too long, or maybe because this was like an unexpected gift, but his senses seemed more highly tuned than normal. This was the closest you got to heaven, he decided through the achingly sweet mist. And the furthest place from hell. This, this, *this*...

She cried out just before he did, tightening her arms around his neck and pulling his head down to kiss him, so that at the moment of abandonment they were locked together in every way that counted. She revelled in the feel of him inside her, the sensation of someone so big and so strong being momentarily helpless, caught in the grip of passion which made his powerful body shudder, and she thought she had never known anything quite so heart-stoppingly beautiful.

Emotions were funny things—they pounced on you at unpredictable times—but a woman was especially vulnerable after lovemaking, and Keri especially so just then. She felt rocked in the aftermath of debilitating pleasure, and then in flooded doubt, insecurity and an aching wistfulness which began to gnaw away at her dreamy state. How heartbreaking that it should have taken her until now to experience something as beautiful as this. She bit her lip.

Jay drew his mouth away and dropped his head heavily onto her shoulder, feeling empty, sleepy. He yawned against her skin and closed his eyes.

Keri felt the steady slowing of his breathing and her heart sank. She wasn't holding out for comfort or reassurance—she just wanted him to say something—anything—even if it wasn't true. For what could *she* say to him, when what had just happened was completely outside her experience?

Encroaching sleep was stalled by the sudden tension in her body, and Jay stifled a sigh. Why could women never let you sleep? Didn't they know that a man was empty—literally empty—after orgasm? That he had lost part of his body during the act and needed to recoup his strength? But he guessed he owed her more than that…she had, after all, been so very, very sweet.

He raised his head, his eyes dazed and smoky, about to murmur his appreciation when he saw her look of utter confusion and he frowned. Please don't come the *we shouldn't have done that* trip on me, he prayed silently.

He stared down at her gravely, his fierce expression warning her not to go down the route of pointless regret.

'Do you always look so uptight afterwards?' he observed softly.

Something in his unspoken censure made her do what she hadn't planned without stopping to think about the consequences. And she told him.

'I'm not sure.' She saw his look of confusion, but it didn't come even close to her own. 'That was the…my…my first time,' she admitted shakenly.

Jay froze. Oh, dear God, no—not that. 'You sure didn't *act* like a virgin,' he stated disbelievingly.

If she had been watching a film the scene might almost have been funny. But it was real, and it was happening to her, and funny was the last thing it was.

She shook her damp hair. 'That wasn't what I meant—of course I'm not a virgin.' But she might as well have been, for all that the other times counted next to this. Her body felt as though it had been steeped in sweet, sticky syrup, but she felt totally defenceless—as though he had touched a part of her that had been a mystery until now.

His eyes narrowed. His thinking wasn't at its best at times like this. 'Your first time?' he repeated carefully. 'What was?'

'My first orgasm,' she said in a small voice. 'Or, rather, my second now.'

CHAPTER SIX

FOR a moment there was complete silence, save for the hissing and spitting of the fire and the thunder of Keri's heart—so loud that it deafened her and surely must him too, when they were still so close and he was still intimately joined to her.

'Say that again,' he instructed softly.

To admit it once had been bad enough, and twice would be toe-curlingly awful, but she guessed it was too late in the day to play coy.

She attempted a shrug, but the truth in this particular case was bald, and no words could infuse it with a soft glow. 'I've never had an orgasm before.'

He withdrew from her abruptly and reached over to haul some blankets from the heap, throwing one over both of them, but he didn't pull her back into his arms, just levered himself up onto his elbow and surveyed her with steady, unblinking eyes.

'You're kidding?'

'You think my sense of humour is that warped?'

'I guess not,' he said slowly.

He leaned over and caught a strand of her hair which was dangling over her cheek. He looped it behind her ear and, stupidly, her stomach went to mush. She was missing him touching her, she realised. Wanting all over again that closeness which had seemed closer than she had been to anyone else—but

79

that was an illusion, brought about by pleasure. She had not been close to him, not really—only in the physical sense, and that wasn't the way which counted.

'How come?' he murmured, seeing the brief tremble which shivered her skin, and he took her into his arms again, sensing that this was more complicated than he had thought. Though when he stopped to think about it he hadn't exactly been doing much *thinking*—had he?

'I'm sure you don't want a catalogue of my disastrous love-life,' said Keri, resisting the urge to snuggle right into him, as though that was an intimacy too far.

'Well, not a blow-by-blow account, that's for sure!' But it was a mistimed attempt at humour. 'Hey,' he said, his voice softening, for her lips were a soft pucker that he found himself wanting to kiss all over again. 'Come here.'

For a moment she was rigid in his arms, like an ice-cube refusing to melt, but then reaction kicked in and she began to dissolve under his touch, and for the first time in her life she realised the true supremacy which could be wielded by a man who brought a woman such heart-stopping pleasure.

The last thing he wanted was some kind of heavy scene on his hands. He dropped a soft kiss on the top of her head. 'You don't have to say anything—not a thing—if you don't want to.'

He was lightly skating his fingertips over her back now, an almost innocent gesture which should not have aroused her, but Keri had tasted pleasure and she was greedy for more.

But that was crazy. Once in the heat of the moment could be understood—but doing it again would be a whole different ball-game. Wouldn't it?

Almost imperceptibly she shifted away from him, so her breasts were no longer pressing into his chest, and Jay felt the tug of desire subside.

'It's just never happened before,' she whispered.

'I find that hard to believe.' He traced the line of her lips with a thoughtful finger. 'Someone as gorgeous as you. I thought men would be busting with a kind of macho pride to show themselves as great lovers.'

Someone as gorgeous as you. Keri supposed that a lot of women might have preened at that, but she had spent her whole adult life having compliments paid about her looks. Overkill—which resulted in them meaning nothing.

And would someone like Jay even begin to understand that what was perceived as physical beauty often got in the way? Men often regarded her as a possession—like a piece of priceless porcelain which must be treated with reverence and respect. And porcelain was cold, whereas she was warm flesh and blood. Or so she had just discovered with him.

Maybe if she hadn't been lying naked with him in front of a fire she might have clammed up, closed the subject completely. But the sudden rattle of the wind against one of the windows reminded her that outside a storm was still blowing and they were completely cut off, blanketed against the outside world, cocooned against the snow in this fire-darkened room. Could anything touch her here except for pleasure itself?

'I think that men are intimidated by me,' she admitted, growing hot with remembered rapture. Her voice was suddenly breathless as she turned her head to look at him. *He* certainly hadn't been intimidated. 'Which makes what just happened all the more amazing.'

There was a long pause while the implications of *that* hit him like a sledgehammer. 'You mean the lowly driver and the beautiful model?' His tone was dry, mocking. 'Not so unusual, I think, Keri. Literature is full of examples of unsuitable couplings—the high with the low, the rough with the smooth.' He ran his fingers over her belly with masterly possession, feeling her shake beneath their practised touch.

'So what was it that really turned you on?' he drawled. 'Are you one of those women who like a bit of rough—with the kind of man you wouldn't normally meet? Or was it the Navy connection—maybe you dream about a man in uniform? A lot of women do, you know, and you may be one of them.'

How had she been so short-sighted as to imagine that she was cocooned from pain and hurt in this place when his words were as wounding as arrows? She tried to push his hand away. 'Stop it—how dare you say those things?'

But he gripped her fingers, curling his own around them in a sensual trap and bringing his face close up to hers, his breath warm and sweet and wine-scented.

'It wasn't meant to be an insult,' he amended on a murmur. 'Just a problem you might like to solve, and then hopefully it won't happen again.' He grinned. 'Or, rather, it will!'

That hurt even more, and for a moment she couldn't figure out why—and then she realised that she had given herself to him passionately and freely, and now here he was, helping her to work out where she had gone wrong before, talking already about a future which did not include him. But it couldn't—she knew that, and so did he. Their lifestyles were oceans apart, their interests probably similarly separate. All they had was a physical compatibility which was almost cruel in its random unsuitability.

'Hey,' he said softly. 'Problems always have solutions, you know—don't look so sombre.'

Her chin came up, suddenly strong, almost defiant. Surely a woman was allowed one indiscriminate love affair in her life? From her back-catalogue of practised smiles, she fished out an I-don't-care one.

'I didn't mean to.'

'Good.' He stroked her cheek and she kissed him, softly and sweetly, and then harder, and deeper.

He groaned. Closed his eyes and let the world dissolve away. He moved his head and heard her catch her breath as the rough rasp of his jaw skated over her breast.

She swallowed as he caught a nipple in between his teeth, nipping and licking at it until she gave a sharp little cry of pleasure.

'Like that?' he murmured.

'No, I hate it.'

He laughed. That was better—easier by far to make love to a woman when she wasn't coming over all helpless.

'Jay, do you…?'

'Do I what?' he questioned thickly, between licks.

She had almost forgotten what she was asking, but then his hand snaked between her thighs again and she knew she must not be led by feeling alone. But it was hard to think of anything other than this hot, dark mist of wanting.

'Do you often do this kind of thing?'

'Funnily enough…' The pad of his thumb circled cool, silky flesh, and he felt her sigh of pleasure against his neck. He smiled as he moved it to where it was more heated, so that her head fell back against the rug. 'I don't often find myself marooned in the snow with beautiful models.'

Which hadn't been what she had been asking at all.

He stopped what he was doing and raised his head to look at her. Her eyes were closed, her expression abandoned and her hair spread out behind her, like a glorious shiny black pillow, and he felt the unexpected leap of his heart. 'If you're asking whether I sleep around indiscriminately,' he said huskily, 'then the answer is no. If you're asking for numbers, then I'd say it was none of your business—just the same as I wouldn't dream of asking you. Is that fair, Keri?'

Fair? She couldn't say, and frankly didn't care, because by now all she wanted was for him to carry on with what he had been doing. She had succumbed to his lovemaking and it wasn't going to last beyond the thaw, when they found their way out or someone found them. He had her in his thrall, and to deny that would be stupid—so why not just lie back and make the most of it?

But it seemed that Jay had other ideas, for once he

had stroked on another condom he effortlessly lifted her up, bringing her right down on top of him, his eyes narrowing as he heard her startled gasp of delight as he filled her.

'Do it to me,' he murmured, on a note of sensual invitation. 'Will you, Keri?' She *was* shy, he saw that now, and he shook his head in a gesture which spoke of both despair and elation. What kind of men had she known in the past?

He smoothed the flat of his hand gently down the side of her hip and saw the look she gave him—a look full of tentative trust and yet fear—and silently he damned his own sex for the way they sometimes took pleasure and left a woman with none. His voice softened. 'Only if you want to.'

He felt so hard inside her, as though he had been made to impale her just like that—the key fitting the lock in a door which had finally swung open.

'Yes, I want to,' she whispered. 'More than anything.'

His laugh was low and full of delight, and he let out a slow breath. 'Oh, me, too,' he murmured. 'Me, too.'

It felt different. Strange but wonderful. And Keri was filled with a suffusing kind of warmth and power as she assumed the dominant position over such a dominating man. She began to move, tentatively at first, seeing what pleased him most and then finding out what pleased her too.

He whispered soft words of encouragement and enticement, and touched his fingers to her breasts, and somewhere along the way she lost her inhibitions completely—taking him with her—wild and free—exulting in the sweet, shared journey—only bending her head to kiss him once she saw the rapture take him over and then felt herself caught up in it too. It overcame her with a force which was unstoppable, and she gasped and gasped until there was no air left in her lungs, shuddering out his name in a shaking voice.

She looked down at him, and their eyes locked in a long and silent moment before he pulled her down into his arms.

For breathless minutes they lay there, his arms wrapped tightly around her damp back. Her skin felt like smooth satin against his fingertips and Jay felt an inexplicable sense of contentment creeping over him. As if he could sleep for a million years, maybe more. For once he didn't fight it, just rested his head against her neck and yawned.

'That's three,' he murmured lazily, and fell asleep.

CHAPTER SEVEN

KERI awoke, naked and aching and glowing beneath a blanket, and batted her eyelids hard in confusion, certain that she must still be sleeping. Cautiously she opened her eyes fully against the sharp light.

Where the hell was she?

Pale winter light filtered down through high stained-glass windows, and the blur of white outside the big picture window was a bank of snow. Snow. And then back forged the memories of the long, erotic night and she turned her head to find the space beside her empty.

Jay.

Gone.

She blinked her eyes against the sun dazzling off the snow, remembering the long, sweet night. He had made love to her over and over again—she had lost count of the times—and just as sleep had finally laid its claim on her she had been aware of him disentangling his arms and getting up. She had felt the warmth of blankets as he had floated them down over her—but their warmth in no way matched up to the heat generated by his body.

'Jay,' she had murmured, on a protest.

'Go to sleep,' he had commanded.

Automatically she smoothed down her hair, her hands drifting to breasts which still tingled from his touch, and she felt the slow creep of colour into her cheeks, uncertain whether it was caused by desire or remorse.

But she wasn't going to feel ashamed—most definitely not. What had happened between them had been beautiful—Jay had said so himself, over and over again through the exquisite night which had followed—and how could something so beautiful ever be wrong?

Because life isn't like that, jeered a little voice somewhere in her head. You can't just take pleasure and expect there to be no outcome; there is always a price to pay.

She sat up, her hair falling down all about her shoulders. Where *was* he? And why on earth should she feel shy about calling out his name when last night she had given herself to him completely? And called it more than once then.

'Jay!'

And suddenly there he was, standing in the doorway, leaning against the doorjamb and surveying her with thoughtful eyes. He was, she noted with a disappointing sinking of her heart, already dressed. The darkening of his jaw made him look even more elemental than he had done the night before, and he just stood there, watching her, a curious and unreadable half-smile on his lips.

She could see for the first time that his eyes were green-grey, the colour of sage—wise and all-knowing, all-seeing. Just what *did* they see? she wondered. *Say something, Jay,* she pleaded silently. *Just say something.*

'Good news,' he said, his mouth relaxing into a smile.

Her heart missed a beat. 'Oh?'

'The power's back on. See.' He lifted his hand and flicked a switch and electric light flooded the room, dazzling her even more than the sun outside, so that she blinked her eyes against the bright artificial light.

She knew she ought to be enthusiastic, but this wasn't the conversation she wanted to have. The power supply was about the last thing on her mind. 'That's good. But could you please turn it off—it's blinding me?' Her voice sounded flat as he did as she asked, and she turned her head to stare unseeingly at the bank of brilliant snow outside.

She had expected him to say…what? That last night had been wonderful? That he wanted to do it all over again? She felt a slow, melting ache as she looked at him, because heaven only knew—*she* did.

But she felt shy again, and unsure of herself—the wild, free woman of last night was now like a cold and distant memory. If he wasn't going to mention it, then should she? Could what have happened between them be classified as a one-night-stand? And, if so, was there some kind of etiquette as to how you behaved afterwards? Because she sure as hell didn't have a clue what it was. She felt like the new child in the playground, where everyone else knew how to play the game and wasn't going to tell her the rules.

He saw the look on her face and ran a few options over in his head. If he went over there and took her in his arms then one thing was certain to happen, and he wasn't sure if that was a good idea, for all kinds of reasons he didn't care to analyse. Because Jay had never been into analysing feelings and he wasn't about to start now.

'You want to wash up?' he suggested slowly.

Her body was slick and redolent of the scent of love, but there was some alien, sentimental part of her that wanted to stay that way—a million miles away from the woman who showered twice a day without fail.

'We have towels?' she asked, babbling the words out as if they mattered.

'We do,' he answered gravely.

She wrapped a blanket around her and rose to her feet—and she of catwalk fame, who could flounce and strut to the insistent beat of the music, now found herself as gangly and as awkward as a newborn foal. If this was what orgasm did for you then you could keep it.

But as she went to walk by him he reached out a hand to catch her waist, drawing her up close to his body, and he felt himself grow hard in an instant. He bent his head so that his breath was warm against her cheek.

'I'd like to do it again too,' he whispered.

Keri closed her eyes, revelling in the nearness of him which awoke every aching sense all over again. 'I never said I wanted to do anything,' she whispered back.

'You didn't have to.' His voice was as soft as butter at room temperature. 'It was written all over your face.'

She heard the arrogance in that statement and tried to pull away from him. Was she really that transparent? Or was that the way all women reacted to him? 'You aren't blaming me this morning for wanting what you wanted so badly yourself last night?'

'Blaming you?' He frowned. 'Are you out of your mind? Of course I'm not blaming you.' He held her tight and she melted against him. 'It was a two-way thing, Keri, and it was pretty amazing—' Which was an outrageous understatement and he knew it. 'But it would be nothing short of irresponsible to go back to bed now.' He glanced over at the heap of rumpled blankets and his eyes gleamed. 'Or at least go back to the floor.'

She couldn't laugh, couldn't move. One word stuck out like a razorblade, half concealed beneath the snow. She looked up at him. 'Irresponsible?'

'Sure.' His eyes narrowed. 'You don't think people are going to be worried? You said you had an appointment last night—who was that with?'

She stared at him blankly, as if he was speaking about another universe entirely, and then she remembered. Oh, Lord! 'David,' she said dully.

David. Yeah, it figured. Jay's mouth flattened and he dropped his arms and let her go, wondering why he should have thought otherwise. 'Well, don't you think that David might be worried?' he questioned coolly.

The fact that he hadn't asked her any questions hurt Keri more than she had expected. She wanted to say *David is just a friend*, but the complete disinterest on his face stopped her stone-dead. He could have asked but he hadn't asked—and the reason for that was as plain as the day.

He *didn't care.*

Jay's mouth thinned into an expression of distaste. So was this David a suitable partner? he wondered. Good for the glamour stuff but a wash-out in bed? His eyes were very clear and hard, and so was his voice.

'He'll have wondered why you didn't show,' he said. 'And presumably he might have heard about the weather conditions and put two and two together and reported you missing? Didn't that occur to you, Keri?'

Nothing had occurred to her at all, bar the touch of his flesh against hers and the kiss of his lips. The outside world might not have existed for all the thought she had given it, cocooned inside in the warm, giving circle of his arms.

Now she felt stupid. And uncomfortable—as if he was judging her.

Keri shrugged her bare shoulders. 'It sort of slipped my mind.'

But there was no complicit gleam of understanding in his eyes, just that same coolness which rivalled the snow outside.

'Then I suggest we make a move to get out of here. You'd better get washed and dressed. I'm going out to see what the roads are like—maybe see if I can dig the car free.'

'You want me to help?'

'No,' he said shortly. 'I work better on my own. Fix us both something to eat and I'll be back as soon as I can.'

Just that, and then he was gone. No long, smoochy kiss or smouldering look promising more passion. Keri shivered as he slammed out of the door and a gust of chill wind blasted its way over her skin.

She found a sliver of soap in the bathroom and washed as best she could, trying to keep her mind on the task in hand and not to let it wander in pursuit of questions which could not be answered. At least she must be grateful for the slow trickle of hot water, which right at that moment felt a million times better than her usual power-shower.

She dressed in yesterday's clothes and went back down to the kitchen, where the leftovers from last night's meal lay congealing in the saucepan. She shuddered and upended them into the bin, then boiled a kettle and made herself a cup of black tea, wondering how long Jay would take and whether he would be successful.

He was gone for the best part of two hours, during which time she washed the dishes and tidied away the blankets in the sitting room. She pulled a book down from the shelf and curled up on the sofa, but she didn't take in a single word of it.

And then she heard the sound of a car drawing to a halt, and moments later Jay came in. His skin was flushed with exertion, fine sweat sheening the strong face, and his eyes were glittering.

Keri sprang to her feet, her heart thundering, searching his face for something—*anything*—but his features were non-committal. She knew that it mocked common sense, but deep down she was praying that they would be stuck here for longer.

'You...freed the car?'

He nodded. 'I did. The sun had softened the snow—

it wasn't difficult. The roads look okay. I think we should make a move—at least to the nearest town.' He paused, having decided on his strategy while he was shovelling snow. 'You can catch a train there.'

She was already disappointed, but at these words her mouth suddenly dried. 'I don't mind travelling with you.'

'No,' he said flatly. 'I don't want to risk it happening again.'

What? she thought, slightly hysterically. The breakdown, or the lovemaking? She saw the quick glance he flicked at his watch. 'You mean you want to leave straight away?'

'In a minute. I'm starving. We'll eat first, and then we'll get going.'

'Eat what?' she questioned steadily. 'You saw what there was.'

There was a heartbeat of a pause. 'We can heat up what we didn't eat last night.' He saw the look on her face and his eyes grew flinty. 'Oh, no.'

Oh, yes. 'I threw it away. We can't eat spaghetti bolognese for breakfast!'

'Brunch.' His eyes were cold. 'So we eat nothing. Is that right, Keri?'

She could feel his rage bouncing off him in almost tangible waves. 'You're angry,' she said flatly.

'Well, what do you expect?' he demanded incredulously. 'I've just been out doing hard labour, which produces real hunger—not the automatic mood to eat at mealtimes which you get from hanging around an office all day. Or the self-imposed denial brought about from trying to maintain an unnaturally low body-weight! Can't you do *anything* practical?'

'I can paint walls,' she said, stung into self-defence.

'Yeah, very useful under the circumstances! Just give that ceiling a quick coat, will you, while we starve to death?'

His contempt was withering—and not, she realised, simply because she had thrown the food away. In a couple of sentences he had managed to dismiss her world, and the standards by which she lived. Well, that should take care of any foolish romantic dreams she might have been in danger of harbouring.

'I'm sorry.' She met his gaze squarely. 'There isn't really a lot else I can say—unless you want me to try to fish it out of the bin for you?'

He looked at her. Since when did missing a meal make him grouchy to the point of unreasonable? Surely not because she'd had a date with a man last night? If she chose to play away then that was up to her—he certainly wasn't into making moral judgements.

And there was no point in parting on bad terms. It had, after all, been pretty…well… He shook his head in slight disbelief. 'Come here,' he said softly, and held out his hand.

A stronger woman might not have taken it, but Keri was not feeling particularly strong right then. Was this the price that you paid for the beauty and the closeness which went with the kind of sex she had shared with Jay? The feeling that he was now somehow *part* of her? As though he had captured something of her and now she belonged to him, unable to shake free the invisible chains which bound them?

You're being fanciful, she told herself. But his mouth was in her hair, and on her neck, his breath hot and warm and rapid, and she felt an instant response, threading her fingers greedily into the tangled thickness of his dark hair.

In an instant he was aroused, but he forced reason to take over from sheer physical desire. He lifted his head and stared down at her, a diamond-hard smile angling his mouth. 'The sooner we get moving, the less chance there is of the police being alerted. Could waste a lot of money if they mount an abortive rescue campaign. Unless, of course, you have a secret fantasy about being winched to safety by a helicopter?'

Keri blinked rapidly. How could he remain so calm and so reasonable, be able to switch off so thoroughly while she was at the mercy of a swirl of emotions which left her reeling?

All she could hear was the pounding of her heart and the swishing rush of her blood. She didn't want to go, or move from this place, and yet clearly he did. And he was right. There were people waiting for them back home who would be beginning to worry—she couldn't just turn her back and pretend they didn't exist.

Yet surely a man of his calibre was wasted, just driving round the country like this? Couldn't his undoubted gifts of strength and resourcefulness be put to some better use? And couldn't she be the one to point him in the right direction? Broach it gently, carefully, she thought. Don't offend his pride or his masculinity.

'Jay?'

Something was coming, and she wasn't about to ask him what he thought the road conditions would be like.

He kept his voice neutral. 'Yes, Keri?'

'It's been...well...'

'Wonderful—yes, it has.' He kissed the tip of her nose.

'And...well, haven't you ever thought that you're— well, *wasted* doing this kind of thing?'

He raised his eyebrows. 'In what way, exactly?'

His face looked so forbidding that she regretted having started, but she couldn't really stop now. 'Well, driving for a living.'

'There's something wrong with driving?'

There was some undercurrent to his voice that she didn't quite understand. 'Oh, there's nothing actually *wrong* with it—'

'Well, thank heavens for that,' he murmured sardonically.

'It's just that you seem to have so much else to offer...' She saw the slight twist of his mouth and rushed on, terrified that he might think she was alluding to his prowess in the lovemaking department. 'I mean your SEAL background, your resourcefulness. The way you got us out of a jam and made the best of it—not a lot of men could do that.'

Which, translated, meant *I want to go to bed with you again.* He kept his gaze steady. 'Well, thanks,' he murmured.

'Someone like you could make a fortune,' she continued softly, 'if you really set your mind to it.'

As in-house stud to beautiful but unfulfilled women like you? he wondered. But he couldn't admit he wasn't tempted—what man wouldn't be? He looked down into the wide dark eyes and thought fleetingly of telling her, and seeing her reaction *then*. But it wouldn't work—it *couldn't* work.

Would he call her up and ask her to dinner? To talk about *what*, exactly? The fact that her mascara had run? That she'd gained a pound? In other words ruin it—and ruin the memory into the bargain. He had told her more than he had intended to, but he could blame the weather and the isolation on that false intimacy.

But women always misinterpreted confidences— which was why he didn't usually fall into the trap of allowing any. They read more into them than they ought to, started thinking things which made him want to run a mile.

He hadn't been lying when he'd told her that it had been wonderful, but it was nothing to do with her world. Or his. And he was pragmatic enough to walk away from something before reality ruined even the memory of it.

'Well, I'll bear that in mind,' he said evenly, and his eyes glittered. 'Any time I'm thinking about a career change.'

Her face had gone very pale, and he was reminded of that look of trust and fear when he had lifted her onto his lap in the middle of the night, and he relented, sliding his fingertips down over the silken skin of her cheek.

'Listen, Keri,' he said. 'What happened last night was great.' His voice became a silken caress. 'You've

proved to yourself that you can have satisfying sex—
you just have to find the right man.'

The words hung on the air as clearly as if he had
painted them on a banner in letters six feet high. *But
that man isn't me.*

She knew that anyway.

A shudder of distaste ran through her. He thought
all she was talking about was physical satisfaction. She
had wanted not to hurt *his* pride and now it seemed
that it was going to take a monumental effort to sal-
vage her own. She pretended that there was a camera
trained close up on her face, and smiled as coldly as
the air outside.

'Didn't you say something about dropping me at the
nearest train station?' she questioned.

He nodded. So she wasn't going to cling. Predict-
ably, he found himself a little disappointed—but
wasn't that just human nature for you? Contrary as
hell—just like he was.

He looked down at her, drinking in the perfection
of her one last time. She looked, he realised, the very
antithesis of the ice queen he had first met—warm and
sensual and alive. Had he done that to her? Brought
life to her sexual desert? He remembered the eagerness
with which she had opened her body to him during
that long, exquisite night and some primitive emotion
flitted across his soul. He wondered why he was feeling some kind of misplaced loyalty to this guy David
she had been due to meet. If a man couldn't bother to
learn how to give a woman pleasure, then surely he
got what he deserved.

And why not complete this assignment himself? 'I

guess I'll catch up with you at the launch,' he said casually.

She had been mentally resigning herself to the fact that this was the last time she would see him, and his words startled her. 'The l-launch?' she stumbled.

'Sure. For the diamond campaign,' he elaborated. 'If you're the face which is about to sell a thousand gems, then won't they expect you to be there?'

Yes, of course they would. A lavish party at one of London's top hotels, which normally she would have considered a necessary duty in the line of work. But now…Keri's heart leapt with excitement and there was nothing she could do to stop it—because she wanted to see this man again more than she could ever remember wanting anything in her life. 'You mean that you've been invited too?' she questioned, equally casually.

'Hardly, sweetheart.' His mouth twisted into an odd kind of smile as he heard the note of surprise in her voice. 'I'll be there guarding the jewellery.'

CHAPTER EIGHT

ARRIVING back in London was like being on a different planet; there had been no snow in the capital other than a brief flurry of flakes which had melted before they touched the pavements. And Keri felt like a different woman from the one who had left there the day before.

She let herself into her apartment to find the Ansaphone flashing. Five messages. But she didn't play them straight away—for once having other things on her mind. She wandered from room to room feeling displaced, as if she were seeing the gleaming apartment for the first time and comparing it to the very basic standard of the house where she had experienced such intense physical love.

Keri shivered.

It was as if Jay had pervaded her senses with a power which seemed to throw everything else into the shadows. Acutely, she could remember the magic of his touch, the hard brilliance of his eyes and the fleeting softness of his features relaxed in the act of love. And she knew she couldn't even think straight until she had washed every trace of him from her body.

She threw a huge handful of her most expensive bath-soak into the tub and submerged herself, right up to her nose, closing her eyes and breathing in the fragrant fumes as she prayed for the glowing ache to leave her.

The messages were from David, her model agency, her sister, her model agency again—yes, the driver had contacted them about the diamonds and would she please let them know she was back safely?—and David again—where the hell was she?

Her head was aching by the time she pressed the 'delete' button. With a slight sense of cowardice she left a message on David's home phone and told him she was safe and would call soon. Then she punched out her sister's number, and the connection was made on the second ring.

In the background, Keri could hear the sound of a toddler screaming. 'Erin?'

'Keri! Thank God! Are you okay?'

Tough call. 'Well, I'm back—safe and sound.'

'What happened? David's been ringing—he said you hadn't showed and that he couldn't get hold of you.'

'I didn't know he had your number.'

'Neither did I. Keri—what the hell has been going on?'

Her whole world had been turned upside down, that was what. 'Can I come over and see you?' she questioned slowly.

'Of course you can. When?'

'I'm on my way,' said Keri grimly.

Her sister lived in the same city, but a few miles away from the expensive centre which Keri inhabited. It was short on parks and green open spaces, and maybe not the ideal place to bring up a young child, but for now it was home. One day, her sister said, she might just do the sensible thing and move to a cheaper and far-flung place in the countryside, but not yet. Erin still had too many memories to be able to bear to tear herself away from them.

Her husband had been killed in a hit-and-run, his life snuffed out like a candle. He had never seen his unborn son, nor lived to achieve the success he had worked so hard for. For a while Keri had thought that Erin might crumble and go under, but she hadn't. Thank God she'd had the baby. Thank God.

The door opened and Erin stood there, her dark eyes narrowed as she stared at her twin.

Nature had given her exactly the same mix from the genetic paintbox as Keri—black eyes, black hair, tall, rangy build—yet the two sisters no longer looked like two peas in pod. Or maybe their experience of life had just made them different.

Erin's hair was tied back in a French plait—her face entirely free of make-up. She was slim, though slightly rounder than Keri, and she rarely wore anything other than her tough workaday uniform of jeans and a shirt.

Her eyes narrowed as she stared at her sister. 'What's happened?' she demanded.

It was that shorthand, that telepathy of someone knowing you so well and so instinctively, who could read your face in an instant. Erin had had it with her husband, but Keri had never had it except with her sister.

'Where's Will?'

'Asleep. Tantrummed-out. So let's make the most of the peace.'

Keri slumped into an armchair and sighed, and then it all came tumbling out. The snowstorm. The breakdown. The man with the grey-green eyes who had been so unfazed by her while she had been dazzled and captivated and infuriated by him in turn.

'And attracted?' questioned Erin shrewdly. 'I mean sexually?'

There was a pause. 'Oh, God, yes. Overwhelmingly.'

The silence spoke volumes.

'So you slept with him.'

It was a statement, not a question, and Keri's head shot up. 'You're shocked?'

'Utterly.' Erin laughed. 'And, no, before you ask—not because I'm making a judgement, but because it's so unlike you!'

'I know it is,' said Keri unhappily.

'And now you've fallen for him big time?'

'I hardly know him.' But something had been forged that night—something she couldn't even come close to explaining, not even to herself.

'So get to know him better! Are you seeing him again?'

'Sort of.' Keri met a pair of eyes identical to her own.

'What's that supposed to mean?'

'He'll be at the diamond launch—it's at the Granchester Hotel, on Saturday.'

Erin frowned. 'As your guest?'

Keri shook her head. 'No. He'll be guarding the jewellery.'

'So it's not a date?'

'Nowhere near a date.' Keri sighed. 'The point is that he didn't ask for one.' Even after everything that had happened between them. Or maybe, she thought, with a sudden painful sense of insight, *because* of what had happened between them.

'You could have asked *him*,' Erin pointed out. 'This is the twenty-first century.

'A woman shouldn't have to,' Keri said stubbornly.

'Oh, Keri!'

'Anyway, it wouldn't work. He's a driver.'

Erin assumed a look of disgust. 'You don't believe all that crap?'

'No,' said Keri slowly. 'But I suspect he does.'

'Maybe that's why he didn't ask,' said Erin. 'And you can't really blame him. Think about it—you're one of the country's top models and he sits behind the wheel of a car for a living! Of course he isn't going to ask you out, because he isn't going to risk what he sees as certain rejection!'

'Despite the fact that we made love?' But the words seemed wrong, as if she was using them to dress up the act, to give it more importance than it actually merited.

'Of course!' Erin scoffed. 'Having a physical compatability is one thing—but going out together throws up all kinds of problems! Maybe he'll be worried about using the wrong knife if he takes you out to eat!'

Keri wanted to tell her sister she'd got it all wrong, that Jay had qualities which superseded his lowly position. Indeed, she'd never met a man so comfortable in his own skin. 'No. He isn't like that,' she said slowly.

'Well, in that case, just wait to see what happens on Saturday.' Erin leaned forward. 'Forgive me for sounding prurient, and you certainly don't *have* to answer this, but some of us live in a sex-free zone these days. Was it...?' Her voice was tentative. 'I mean, was it...good?'

There wasn't possibly anyone else in the world she would have told—except Jay, of course—but her sister was her own flesh and blood, and closer than close.

'Oh, Erin, it was the best,' she said simply. 'The very best...ever.'

There was silence for a moment, and then Erin nodded. 'Then maybe he's liberated you at last, Keri,' she said gently. 'And now you're free to find yourself a real relationship with someone else.'

Without intending to her twin had made it all sound like a question of mechanics—as if fulfilment was what it was all about. So was it? When something like that happened—did it bind you close to a man, even if he was the wrong man? And wouldn't it sound crazy to admit to her sister that she didn't want anyone else other than a sloe-eyed stranger who had made her feel like a real woman?

She drank tea and helped her sister make cupcakes, and when Will woke up Keri went upstairs to him. His bedroom was a bright, colourful and adventurous room—she had decorated it herself, in blues and greens, and painted a mural of the seashore on one wall.

His sleepy eyes blinked open and he held his arms

up, and Keri snuggled her little nephew tightly to her, closing her eyes and breathing in the warm, clean, child-like scent of him. She loved him dearly, though often she looked at Erin's dark-ringed eyes and wished he wouldn't run her so ragged, and today it was as if all her senses were sharpened—as if someone had left them raw and open and she saw his innocence and beauty as never before.

It was dark by the time she arrived home, and she walked slowly into her bedroom. The flat was quiet and dimly lit, and she hugged her arms tightly around herself, closing her eyes and wishing that Jay was here and that they were his arms.

And wondering how she could bear to wait until Saturday to see him again.

CHAPTER NINE

JAY hadn't realised he was waiting. Waiting was not in his nature; he was a man of action, not contemplation. But the moment he saw her walk into the crowded ballroom, he expelled a soft breath of expectation.

The ice-queen was back. Big-time.

Had the agency told her what to wear? Or did she normally attend functions like this—dripping in diamonds with a satin dress so clinging that it looked like gleaming black skin?

Probably. The room was full of beautiful women, all dressed up to the nines, but he couldn't stop staring at Keri, and his appetite was sharpened by the fact that she did not look his way. Not once. Which whetted his appetite even more.

Was she regretting that long and beautiful night?

Jay watched from the perfect vantage point as she drifted into the room and assorted bigwigs and flunkies began to lavish attention on her. He watched while someone took her wrap and someone else handed her a glass of champagne. He stood as silent and as still as a statue beside the glass-fronted cases containing a king's ransom worth of jewels. His heart was beating hard and loud and steady. And then at last she turned her head and stared straight into his eyes.

Keri felt the breath catch at the back of her throat.

He was wearing black jeans, which clung almost indecently to the hard, muscular shafts of his thighs, and a black roll-neck sweater. His jaw was shadowed and dark and his sage eyes were hooded.

Compared to every other man there—all resplendent in their black ties and shockingly expensive suits—he looked about as basic as could be. If she'd needed the perfect illustration of how very different their two worlds were then it was right there, but somehow she didn't care. Because he looked all man—the only man in the room who looked capable of breaking a door down and rescuing a woman. And then making love to her in a way guaranteed to ensure that she would never forget him.

She did her best not to react, not outwardly in any case, but inside her heart was hammering away so violently at her ribcage that she was certain it would be seen through the slippery silk-satin of her gown.

He was looking right at her. The dress she wore was normal for this kind of function, and it moulded itself to her body as if it had been sprayed on. She wore no bra, just two strategically placed pieces of tape which made her small breasts seem to defy gravity, yet she was no more revealingly clothed than any other woman in the room.

So how come she felt completely naked under Jay's scrutiny?

Her cheeks flushing, she turned away to talk to someone before he could see them.

She moved around the room, being introduced to the movers and shakers by the managing director of the diamond firm. Her photo was everywhere—the isolated backdrop of snow had been stunning, as the art director had intended—but all Keri could think about was that a few hours after those photos had been taken she had been naked in Jay's arms, crying out with amazed pleasure.

He hadn't moved from the spot where he was standing, and after half an hour of looking everywhere but there she could stand it no longer. She grabbed a second glass of champagne and wandered over to him.

'Well, hello again,' she said, with a smile she hoped wasn't too unsure. She held the glass out towards him. 'Drink?'

He shook his head. 'No, thanks. I'm driving.'

'Oh.' Now she felt stupid, standing there with both hands full, and maybe he realised that, for he took the glasses from her and put them on the tray of a passing waitress. Did he have an uncanny knack, she wondered, of knowing exactly what a woman wanted at any given time?

'Better?' he murmured.

'Much,' she lied, because 'better' would be the ability to clear the room completely and have the two of them standing there alone. And then, because this situation was so bizarre and unsettling, she gave him a glassy kind of smile. 'Enjoying yourself?'

In a way. The situation was certainly better than before—but maybe that was because she was about as good to look at as he could imagine. 'I'm working. I'm not here to enjoy myself.'

'Shall I go away again, then?'

'No.' He gave a brief smile. 'Did you come alone?'

'I...well, yes.'

A dark brow was raised in question. 'David not here?'

She looked him straight in the eyes, mesmerised by the soft grey-green light. 'David's just a friend.'

'Is he, now?' he questioned softly. Poor David. But her answer changed things, and Jay gave the stealthy smile of a circling predator. 'Maybe we could go for coffee…or something, when it finishes?'

She would have been a liar if she hadn't admitted to being tempted, because she knew that coffee was the last thing he had in mind, and the sight of him was making all kinds of erotic possibilities lick into life. Her mind flicked through a possible scenario. Would he offer to take her back to some tiny flat on the outskirts of the city with only one thing in mind? Or maybe he would suggest going back to her place, where the differences between them would be so glaringly obvious that it might inhibit both of them? She tried to imagine him climbing into her bed, with its rose-scattered brocade counterpane, and that was when her imagination gave up on her.

Had she really thought that things could be as they had been in the cottage, when the reality of their normal lives was so different?

And Keri realised something else in that moment. That it might be the twenty-first century, and women were supposed to be equal to men, but in something they most definitely were not. She did not want a relationship that was based completely and solely on sex. Once had been spontaneous and gorgeous, but anything else on the same terms would be nothing short of seedy.

She gave him a cool look. 'Sorry. I'll be tired by then.'

He would have suggested a remedy for tiredness, but he could see from the chilly expression on her face that she was no longer the accessible woman he had seduced. He realised that she was about to walk away. So, was the sight of his tough, practical persona in a room full of the glitterati enough to have given her second thoughts?

He saw the faint colour which had washed over her high cheekbones and the hectic glitter of her eyes. No, it was not. 'How about lunch?' he suggested.

Keri blinked up at him in surprise. 'Lunch?'

'I think we've established the fact that you *can* eat, given the motivation.'

She felt the sudden quickening of her pulse. Had he deliberately said that to remind her of the sensual food-fest they had indulged in?

But lunch wasn't seedy—lunch was civilised— though he did somehow stretch the definition of the word civilised. And it was certainly safer than dinner.

'I can do lunch,' she agreed.

'Monday?'

'Why not?'

'I know a place in Docklands, overlooking the wa- ter. It's pretty, and it's close to where I work.'

So he was seeing her on his lunchbreak! Keri let out a small sigh of relief. An hour would mean lunch and only lunch, with no time for anything else. And most people were like Jay, she reminded herself. They worked normal hours with normal restraints. 'We could just go for a sandwich, then,' she said understandingly.

He gave a small smile. 'There's a place called Carter's on the river—do you know it?'

She shook her head. 'No, but I can find it.'

'Okay. I'll see you in there at one.' He slid his hand into the back pocket of his jeans and withdrew a card. 'Here's my number—call me if you get held up.'

As she took the card from him their fingers brushed and it was electric, her skin tingling with just that brief contact. Her head jerked up and she saw the inky dilation of his eyes in silent response. Did this happen for him with all women? she wondered desperately. Could he make them melt with a single touch?

'I'll see you at one,' she agreed, and walked away from him, back across the ballroom, her heart thundering with excitement as she asked herself if she was walking straight into trouble.

It felt like the first date she had ever been out on. On Sunday night Keri had slept badly and woke as soon as it was light, and, terrified of going back to sleep and not leaving herself enough time, she overcompensated and arrived in Docklands with an hour to spare.

The winter weather was unforgiving. A soft, cold haze of rain ruled out a pre-lunch walk, she thought, looking out at the troubled waters of the Thames. There was no art gallery close enough to while away the minutes and no shops to wander aimlessly around. Maybe he could shift his lunchbreak around? Oh, what the hell.

She pulled her mobile out of her pocket and tapped in his number. He picked it up on the second ring.

'Jay Linur.'

'Jay? It's Keri. The traffic was better than I thought and I'm here—is there any chance you could knock off a little early?'

There was a pause.

'Why don't you come up to the office?' he said at last. 'I have some paperwork which I must get done.'

'Okay,' she said, wondering if he had deliberately tried to make himself sound important. Paperwork! What paperwork did he have that couldn't wait—his timesheets? 'Tell me where to find you.'

Jay put the phone down and frowned.

'Andy!' he called. 'I'm expecting someone.'

Keri found the building easily and took the stairs rather than the elevator to find herself in a large office which was high-ceiled and wonderfully dimensioned. True, the walls were dull and dingy, but the reflected light from the river helped, and the view of the swirling waters from the windows was spectacular.

An enormous man with the widest pair of shoulders Keri had ever seen crinkled up his blue eyes as she walked in. 'Hi.' He smiled. 'Jay's expecting you.' He clicked an intercom button on his desk. 'She's here, boss!'

Jay silently cursed, and then said, 'Send her in.' How many times had he told Andy to lose the handle by which he had been known for years?

'Go right through.' Andy grinned, pointing to the door of an inner office.

Keri's forehead pleated in a small frown. Boss?
'Thanks.'

She walked into the inner sanctum and it was not
what she was expecting—though, to be honest, what
exactly *had* she been expecting?

Jay was seated behind an impressive wooden desk,
the sleeves of his dark sweater rolled up and a com-
puter quietly humming away. Behind him was a map
of the world, and there were lots of different coloured
pins stuck in it. It looked, she thought suddenly, like
a powerhouse. As if this was a place which mattered
and he was a person who mattered.

Something didn't add up.

She stared at him.

'Hello, Keri.' Her hair was tied back like a schoolgirl's and she wore a knee-length leather coat, with
long boots to match. She was very fond of leather, he
thought, and the hot kick of lust became as scorching
as the desert.

She looked around the office again. 'Would you
mind telling me what's going on? Why did that man
call you boss?'

He guessed he could play the evasion game for as
long as it took, but what would be the point?

'Because I am. It's my company. I own it. I supply
the drivers, and the guards, and private investigators
too.' He didn't mention his significant portfolio of
property. That might have seemed like a little too
much information all at once.

It was like having a gauze curtain whisked away
from her eyes so that her vision suddenly became
crystal-clear. Of course. Of *course.* It all began to

make perfect sense now—why things had not quite added up.

The confident, almost arrogant way he had behaved towards her when most men were slightly intimidated. His knowledge of French wines. You didn't need to wear fancy clothes or splash money around to prove you were a rich man—sometimes success could just ooze from every pore—and, my God, it certainly oozed from him.

'You…you lease these offices?'

'Well, I own them, actually. There are a couple more on the floor beneath.'

Her eyes widened as the significance of *that* sank in. Offices in this part of London didn't come cheap. 'You aren't a driver at all, are you, Jay?' she said quietly.

He met the accusation full-on. He could see the sudden stiffening of her body, but worse than that was the fleeting look of hurt which clouded her big dark eyes. As if he'd betrayed her. Hell, one night in her arms and she was acting as if he owed her something! 'Well, that's not strictly true—'

The confusion began to evaporate and anger took over—and in a way that helped dissolve the feeling that he had left her looking like a fool. 'Oh, please don't play with words! I'm not doubting your ability to drive a car!' She drew in an angry little snort of breath. 'Did it amuse you to deliberately deceive me?'

'I did *not* deliberately do anything. Why would I want to deceive you? Don't read more into it than there was, Keri—one of my drivers went off sick at the last minute so I stood in for him.'

'Why didn't you tell me that at the time?'

'Why on earth should I?' He gave a slightly incredulous smile. 'Can you just see the scenario if I'd suddenly just announced it to a client? *Hi, my name is Jay, and actually what you see isn't really what you get. I'm not a driver; I own the company!* How crass would that have been?'

'You're missing the point!'

'Am I?' His gaze was very steady as he moved across the room towards her. 'I fail to see how. Would you have treated me differently if you'd known?' He gave a slow smile as he remembered the way she had treated him. 'Maybe that would have been something worth telling you for!'

'That is cheap!'

He shook his head as he allowed himself the rare luxury of recall. How long had it been since *that* had happened? A woman taking him on the most basic terms of all, without trappings or status? 'No, it's true,' he contradicted softly.

She backtracked through her memory. Maybe he hadn't actually told her any lies, but he must have been laughing fit to burst—especially when she had falteringly suggested that he was wasted as a driver and he might be able to find other work. 'Did it give you pleasure to masquerade as something you weren't?' she demanded bitterly.

'Of course it didn't give me pleasure!' He sighed, held the palms of his hands up in a gesture of peace. 'It just seemed irrelevant at the beginning, and if I'd told you during or afterwards then it might have seemed like boasting. As if I was trying to impress you with what I was rather than who I was.' And hadn't playing his wealth down become second nature?

She glared at him. 'Well, if you're so bloody rich then I suggest you do something about these offices—I've never seen anything so dingy in my life!'

He started laughing. 'Are we still on for lunch?'

'I've lost my appetite!'

'No change there, then.'

She didn't smile back. 'Very funny.'

He was aching to take her in his arms, but something in her eyes was warning him off—and in a way that excited him almost as much as it frustrated him. 'Have you any work lined up?' he asked suddenly.

Keri narrowed her eyes. 'Why?'

'Is that a yes or a no?'

'I have a...' She wasn't about to start telling him about the lingerie contract—she could just imagine his reaction to *that*. 'A job in a few weeks' time.' Other than that she was free—a welcome space in her workload after jobs being booked back-to-back for months.

'And in the meantime? What do you normally do in between jobs?'

She filled in her time as usefully as possible, that was what she did. She visited galleries and friends, and shopped and saw films. 'Depends.'

My, but she was paying him back for his supposed 'deception'. 'Do you want to do something for me?'

Her suspicious body-stance did not alter. 'Like what?'

'Why not paint my offices?' He saw her mystified look and it amused him. 'Is it such a crazy idea?' he mused. 'You told me that you're good at it. You told me that was what you originally wanted to do, and you've just torn the place to pieces. You're right—they are dingy.'

The suggestion pleased her more than it had any right to. It was, she realised, a way to maybe find out who the real Jay Linur was. And a chance to show him that she was not just some mindless clotheshorse who paraded in front of the camera. To show him what she could do—maybe more importantly to prove to *herself* what she could do.

She stared at him. 'Why, Jay?'

Because I want to make love to you again. Because you've left me with a fever in my blood and I need a little saturation therapy to make it go away. But maybe it was more than that. There had to be more to life than standing in a snowy field in the middle of winter wearing very little. Hadn't she said so herself?

He shrugged. 'You told me you sometimes were bored with standing in front of a camera, that interior design was what you planned before modelling came out and grabbed you—so why not explore it as an option? I can be your first legitimate assignment, if you like.'

Keri stared at him, at the grey-green eyes which were surveying her quizzically. He was offering her an opportunity to do something different, allowing her to indulge the creative side of her nature, but it wasn't that which was making her mouth dry with excitement.

She knew deep down that they would be lovers again—she wasn't that self-deluding. But this time she wasn't going to make it easy for him—not in any way. Sex wasn't supposed to be a battle, but even so she had given in too easily before. If Jay Linur wanted her then he was going to have to try a whole lot harder.

'So what's your answer?' he questioned softly.

'You'll give me a free hand?' she verified.

'Free as you like, sweetheart,' he agreed, but once again his body began to ache.

CHAPTER TEN

JAY'S motorbike zipped through the heavy late-morning traffic, the rain buffeting against him, the thunder-laden clouds matching his mood of expectation and anticipation.

She was there, in his office, putting into practice his crazy idea. He knew this because he had already received a phone call from Andy, asking did Jay know that the dishy broad had arrived bearing enough paint to cover the front of Buckingham Palace?

The unspoken question had been why Jay had not bothered mentioning it to his right-hand man. Maybe that was a classic case of denial—of not wanting to admit what he found hard to admit to himself.

He had let a woman onto *his territory*. Not just any woman, either, but a woman *he had had sex with*! For the first time in his life he had allowed desire to blind him to sense.

And he had no one to blame but himself.

He had done some work at home in order to be out of the way when she arrived—he hadn't felt quite ready to lay on the red carpet treatment for her himself—and by the time he'd parked the bike and removed his helmet and made his way upstairs he could hear Andy chatting.

Andy—*chatting*?

The two men had been SEALS together. They had

trained and fought side-by-side, seen the very worst of life and made light of it afterwards. They had wreaked havoc behind enemy lines and then left without a trace. Jay had spent much of his adult life with the tough ex-commando, but he had never once heard him *chatting* like that.

But then she was, he realised suddenly, very easy to talk to.

He walked into the office to be greeted by the sight of a pert bottom leaning over the desk and pointing out something on a chart to Andy, who had clearly never heard the expression eating-out-of-her-hand.

'Well, hello,' Jay said softly.

Andy stopped mid-sentence, and Keri stopped what she was doing, and they both turned round—Andy jumping back from the paint chart as if it had been alive. For a big man, he could certainly move fast!

Jay stood there, his helmet under one arm, the thumb of his other hand hooked into a loop on his trousers, his stance both watchful and territorial, like some latter-day cowboy. Did he do it *deliberately*? she wondered. Decide just what would be the number-one female fantasy and then become its very personification?

He was dressed completely in soft black leather. Leather trousers which clung to the long, lean shafts of his legs and a close-fitting leather jacket. With his black hair and shadowed jaw, the only colour relief came in the grey-green glitter of colour from between the thick forest of eyelashes.

'Good morning, Jay,' she said brightly. 'Though not a very nice one, is it?

He groaned. 'You're not going to be cheerful in the mornings, are you?'

'Probably by *your* standards, yes,' she said innocently, and saw Andy fail to hide a smile. 'I've tried a few patches of paint on the walls of your office—like to have a look at them?'

Surprisingly, his mood had started to lift by a fraction—but then she sure beat Andy on the decorative front. Paint-splattered baggy denim dungarees were proving far more appealing than they should have done—but then he knew only too well what lay beneath.

'I guess so,' he growled, and began to walk towards his office. 'Come on through. Coffee, please, Andy.'

'Sure.'

Keri dawdled for a minute, turned to Andy, and smiled. 'Thanks for all your help.'

His eyes crinkled at the corners. 'My pleasure, ma'am.'

Andy was very definitely American—where Jay only had the hint of a drawl, his was the real thing. They'd been in the SEALs together, so he'd told her. He had bright blue eyes and hair the colour of shadowed corn, and the oddly gentle manner which big men sometimes had.

'Keri!' called Jay's voice impatiently. 'Are you coming in here or not?'

'Demanding, isn't he?' she murmured, half to herself, as she went into the inner sanctum. She had been busy preparing the room before she started painting, though not as busy as she might have expected. Most rooms had some degree of clutter and personal effects, but Jay's had precisely none. No photos. No cute paperweights. No pictures on the walls. There wasn't even a dying pot plant as so often seen in the workplaces of lone men. Nothing. A functional room for a functional man.

Jay was standing in the middle of the room, staring incredulously at the wall next to the window which had a splodge of colour on it—a bright, vibrant red.

He turned around, seeing her dark eyes widened in expectation, like a little girl who had spent all night making a gift for the teacher.

'Is this some kind of joke?' he questioned, in a strangled kind of voice.

'You don't like red?'

'I don't like sitting in a room which looks like someone has been flinging ketchup at the walls.'

'It isn't finished yet,' she said helpfully.

Silently, he counted to ten. 'I may not be Van Gogh, Keri, but I'd kind of worked that out for myself. It's not the lack of application I'm objecting to—it's the damn colour!'

'What's wrong with red? The sky outside is blue, the paintwork white and, given your dual nationality, I thought it would conjure up images of both the British and American flags!'

He looked at her. 'Are you trying to be funny?'

'No.' She shook her head. 'Honestly, Jay—I think it will look stunning—and you *did* tell me I had a free hand!'

'That's because I thought you were just going to brighten it up with the same colour.'

'And what? Paint it *magnolia*? Although it was difficult to make out just what colour it was under the layers of grime—which I am going to have to scrub before I can start.' She gave an exaggerated shudder. 'Places of work should be inspirational, and you won't get much if you're sitting surrounded by a colour which looks like the inside of a milk bottle. Trust me—it will look fine by the time I've finished.'

There was silence for a moment. If he wanted inspiration he wasn't going to start looking for it in his office! Was now the time to enlighten her that places of work were supposed to be just that? And how come they sounded like a pair of newlyweds sparring over the décor for their first home?

'And if it doesn't?'

She heard the dangerous note in his voice. 'Then I'll paint it back exactly the colour it was!' And saw the dangerous look in his eyes. He really *could* be a Big, Bad Wolf.

While she had been chatting she had learnt just how successful the company was. It seemed that Jay was a very wealthy man. Yet, oddly enough, that didn't change her feelings for him one jot. She had been ensnared by him when she'd thought he had very little—so what difference did it make that he actually had a great deal?

He was still looking at her in a way designed to make the steadiest hand drip paint all over the floor, and that was hardly the best way to begin. 'Maybe I'd better begin on the outside office,' she said thoughtfully.

Jay didn't know which was more infuriating—the fact that Keri was innocently painting in the next door office, or the fact that Andy kept whistling. Tunelessly. He hadn't heard him whistle like that for a long time.

He kept out of the way until lunchtime and then stole silently into the outer office. To his surprise, almost one large wall had already been painted blue—the same colour as the sea when you started to go really deep. It was a beautiful colour, but not one he would have considered putting on a wall.

Keri was sitting perched on the desk, with a blob of paint on her nose and Andy looking up at her like a lost puppy dog who had just found its owner. A muscle flickered in Jay's cheek as some inexplicable irritation flared.

'Aren't you going out for sandwiches?' he questioned tersely.

Andy glanced at his watch in surprise and levered his long frame out of the chair. 'Is that the time?' He turned to Keri. 'And what would you like, princess?'

Jay gave a tight smile. *Princess?*

'Oh, don't bother about me,' said Keri quickly. 'I don't normally bother with lunch.'

'She'll have the same as me,' said Jay firmly, and met her eyes. 'There's no way you're starving yourself—understand? You're not standing around having your photo taken now, Keri—this is real work, and I certainly don't want you fainting on the job.'

She felt pretty faint as it was, and that had nothing to do with *real* work. Now that Jay had peeled off his leather jacket he was treating her to the sight of a black T-shirt clinging to all the right places. Keri swallowed. Maybe a sandwich wasn't such a bad idea after all.

Might send the blood rushing to her head and her stomach instead of all the wrong places. 'Thanks. Sounds good.'

The silence seemed immense while Andy grabbed his jacket and put it on, and after he had left it seemed even bigger. Keri seemed aware of every sound in the universe—the faint cry of seagulls outside, the occasional blast of a ship's horn. And her heartbeat. That was absolutely deafening, especially now, because he was strolling across the room towards her, a lazy smile on his lips.

'Do you realise we haven't said hello properly?' he questioned silkily, and pulled her into his arms.

She had been practising for just this moment, and had planned to resist, but now—faced with the reality—resistance flew straight out of the window.

'Hello, Jay,' she said pertly.

He allowed himself a small smile. 'Ah, Keri,' he murmured, brushing his mouth tantalisingly over hers. 'Haven't you been wanting to do that all morning?'

She had been trying her best not to think about it, with varying degrees of success. 'I've actually been concentrating on my painting,' she managed.

'And just how do you concentrate on painting?'

'I...oh, God...I don't *know*,' she gasped, as he flicked his tongue out and teased it against her lips, and she closed her eyes and gave in, wrapping her arms tightly around his neck and pressing her body to his.

He groaned, sliding his hand down over her dungarees and cupping her breast through the rough denim. 'I must have been out of my mind,' he whispered. 'Thinking that I could have you anywhere near me and even think straight, let alone do any work.'

She jerked her head back with a monumental effort. 'Well, you're going to have to try,' she said shakily. 'Otherwise your business will go bust and you'll blame me.'

'I want you.' He drifted his hand further down and heard her moan.

Someone had to stop this and it had better be her, since Jay's eyes were smoky with the kind of desire which was reminding her all too vividly of what he was like as a lover. Any minute now and she wouldn't be able to resist anything.

'The…the wanting has never been in any question,' she agreed firmly. 'But, Jay, we mustn't.'

'Mustn't what?' He dipped his head to trail a featherlight kiss along the line of her jaw. 'We aren't doing anything.' He nuzzled again. 'Just kissing.'

But it was more than that. At least for her it was. This warm sense of homecoming, as if no place in the world could be more perfect than in Jay's arms. And this kind of kisses could lead you to only one place if you weren't very careful. Look what had happened before.

'Andy will be back in a minute.'

'It's his lunch-hour. I'll tell him to go take a walk in the park.'

'It's the middle of winter!' she protested.

'Oh, Andy's tough,' he said easily. 'Like me. We're used to the elements, sweetheart. He'll understand.'

For one second she was tempted as she imagined an erotic way of spending the rest of the lunch-hour.

Jay had awoken in her a voraciously hungry sexual appetite and she would have liked nothing more than to feed it.

But then what? She would have to field Andy's curious and knowing stares all afternoon and live with the feeling that where Jay was concerned she was in danger of always selling herself short. She wasn't going to use sex as a weapon or a tool, but she needed her self-respect as well as his respect—and a quick bout of lovemaking in between coats of paint wasn't designed to help achieve that. Either they did things properly, or not at all.

She shook her head. 'No, Jay.'

He gave a faintly disbelieving moan. 'Are you trying to drive me out of my mind?'

'There wouldn't be a lot of point, would there? Not when you just told me you're already losing it!'

Reluctantly, he laughed and let her go, which made the aching slightly less intense, but his eyes glittered with curiosity. 'So what had you planned? To keep me at arm's length?'

'Certainly during working hours,' she said steadily.

He heard the underlying message. 'You want to go out later?'

It was unbelievable how he broke all the normal rules of conventional behaviour and managed to get away with it. She had heard invitations phrased far more elegantly, but she had never been so excited by one before.

Yet she had vowed not to make it too easy for him, and if she went out with him tonight would she honestly be able to resist him?

He observed her hesitation. 'Or are you ''busy'' tonight?' he suggested mockingly.

Determinedly, she made herself focus on a pile of bills waiting to be paid. 'I'm afraid I am.'

'Oh, I see.' Suddenly the air became full of tension. 'That's your plan, then, is it, Keri?' he questioned softly. 'To tempt and taunt me and ultimately to tease me, by saying no?'

His bad-tempered response made her realise that her instinctual refusal had been the right thing to do. She raised her eyebrows.

'My, my, my—is that always your reaction when a woman turns you down?'

He was frustrated, and temporarily wrong-footed, but not shortsighted enough to point out that it was the first time it had ever happened. 'So you aren't going to go out with me?'

She paused just long enough to give him doubts. 'Not tonight, no. Ask me again.'

So beautifully sure of herself. Had she read all those rulebooks which told you that to hook a man you had to play games—never be free and never return his calls? Because if she was holding out for commitment she was in for a disappointment.

'I'm not a man who likes waiting,' he warned her darkly.

His arrogance fuelled her indignation and she shrugged her shoulders. 'Then don't wait,' she answered coolly. 'Go ahead—ask someone else. And now, if that's everything—I'm going out.'

He watched her grab her coat from the hook, his

eyes drinking in her graceful beauty with admiration.
She must have been reading some book—because if
there was anything which made him want something
it was being told that he might not be able to have it.

CHAPTER ELEVEN

KERI quickly learnt that she didn't like to be kept waiting either, and Jay made her wait three days before he asked her out again. Three days which were an agony of excitement and expectation and fear that he might have decided against it. Three days during which time she learnt that he liked his coffee black, his bread brown, that he worked non-stop and that he wouldn't take telephone calls from a woman called Candy.

'Who's Candy?' asked Keri casually, as she carefully tore off a piece of masking tape.

'Just some broad,' replied Andy. 'One of many.'

Maybe her face remained quizzical.

'Like moths to a flame,' he added with a rueful kind of look. 'But half the time he doesn't notice.'

Or doesn't care? she wondered.

When Andy went out to fetch sandwiches at lunchtime, Jay wandered through, rubbing his eyes and stifling a yawn.

'Late night?' murmured Keri, but she felt the powerful tug of jealousy.

'Late-night call to the States.' His eyes drifted over her. 'You have paint on your nose.'

'Paint everywhere,' she agreed steadily.

I'd like to see it. 'So, are we going out together tonight?'

'I thought you were tired.'

His eyes widened by a fraction. 'Suddenly I'm wide awake.'

She'd done the self-respect thing. Now surely she could relax a little. 'Okay, then.' She smiled up at him and suddenly ached to put her arms around him. 'What would you like to do?'

I think we both know the answer to that, sweetheart. 'You choose.'

She wanted something normal. Something which didn't involve her gazing into his eyes and thinking how bloody gorgeous he was. 'How about a film—we could grab a bite to eat afterwards?'

'A film?'

'You know. Man and woman go to into large, darkened room. Man and woman watch story told on big screen—popcorn optional.'

He gave a reluctant laugh. It wouldn't have been number one on *his* list. 'Okay—why not?'

'Anything in particular you'd like to see?'

He shook his head. 'You choose.

The door opened and Andy reappeared, carrying a brown bag full of food.

Jay's first thought was that this wasn't proving quite as simple as he had anticipated.

And his second was one of suspicion.

All he had wanted was to take her to bed—so how come he'd agreed to see a film with her? He hadn't been to the movies with a woman for years.

The night was dark, but there were no stars. That was the trouble with cities, thought Jay—too much manmade light which killed the natural beauty of the heavens. The neon lights of the cinema complex made Keri's face look ghostly and unreal.

'Did you enjoy it?' she asked.

'It was okay,' he said. 'Though I'm not crazy about subtitles.'

'Because you didn't need them, unlike me.' She looked up at him. 'It isn't just wine labels that you read, is it, Jay? You understood the entire dialogue of the film. You speak French.'

'People do, particularly in Paris,' he mocked.

'But you weren't raised in Paris,' she mocked back. 'So how come?'

'Because I spent the first few years of my life in New Orleans, and then whichever parent I happened to be with at the time insisted I keep my French—so I went to schools where the teaching was bilingual.' He flicked her a smile. 'Maybe we should go and eat now.'

It was a conversational cut-off, presumably as a way of avoiding elaborating on a childhood which sounded awfully disruptive. Maybe it was his way of saying that he had told her things about himself when they were marooned in the house, but now things were different. She wasn't hungry, but she wasn't risking any more barbs about her lack of appetite, so she nodded anyway. 'Sounds good.'

'Where do you want to go?'

'I suggested the film, why don't you decide the food?'

There was a pause, and he touched her cheek with the tip of his finger, snaking it down in a spine-tingling little spiral. 'But you might not like my suggestion, Keri.'

She shivered at his touch. 'Try me.'

'I don't want anything to eat,' he said evenly. 'At least, not yet. I want to take all your clothes off and run my hands over your body and make you gasp and cry again.'

He couldn't see the hot colour which had flushed into her cheeks, nor hear the frantic clamour of her heart. She could look outraged, shocked, appalled. She could refuse and hail a cab. All those choices available to her, and what did she do?

She smiled a slightly shaky smile. 'I have a fridge full of food.'

But he was already lifting his arm for a taxi.

The ride back to her apartment was conducted in a tense and expectant silence. He didn't touch her, nor did he say a word, and Keri's emotions felt as churned up as cake mix. Was it right that this should feel almost *clinical*? But that was down to Jay. Given the choice, she would be snuggled up in his arms, smothering his face with tiny little kisses. Not sitting at either end of the seat, as if they were on their way to a business conference.

She was barely aware of him paying the cab, or of their swift journey to her front door, only that once it was closed behind them they fell on each other with a wild kind of hunger.

He pushed her coat from her shoulders and it fell to the floor, and she found herself frantically unbuttoning his shirt, sliding her hands up underneath the

T-shirt he wore beneath and moaning when she made contact with the silken flesh.

Something hot exploded inside his head. It was all buttons and lace and hardness, and achingly moist softness too. With some last vestige of sanity he groped into his pocket for protection and stroked it on, then kicked his trousers off impatiently. Her panties were down by her ankles, and he pushed her up against the wall and parted her thighs, and her mouth sought his, sucked greedily on his lips as he lifted her up and drove into her with a low, exultant cry torn from his lips.

He tried to slow it down, but it was impossible— *she* was impossible, urging him on with little pleas and moans until she dragged her mouth away from his. He felt her tense, her back arching, and only when he felt her begin to shudder around him could he finally let go, in an orgasm which seemed to go on and on and on.

Through the slowing and muffled beat of her heart, Keri let her damp face fall heavily to his shoulder. 'Shouldn't I at least have offered you a drink first?' she questioned, her voice as sleepy as a well-fed cat.

Jay closed his eyes and locked his arms tightly around her waist. 'You are amazing,' he murmured. 'Completely and utterly and unbelievably amazing. Which way's the bedroom?'

'What bedroom's that?' she whispered. 'You've got me so I can't think straight.'

He tilted up her chin. 'How about a rough idea?' he drawled.

'Keep going, and I'll tell you when to stop.'

He picked her up, a smile playing at the corners of his mouth as he stared down into her eyes. 'Well, I guess there's a first time for everything!' he commented wryly.

He took her to bed, only this time he made love to her as if he had all the time in the world, slowly whispering his fingertips all over her skin, making her feel as if she had only ever been briefly acquainted with her body before, and now he was introducing her to it properly for the first time.

He teased and stroked, tipped her almost to the edge of desire, then drew her back again, time after time, the flow building towards some inexorable peak, frustration growing alongside excitement until finally she begged him not to stop. He gave a small, low laugh of pleasure, as though that had been what he had been waiting for all along. Through the tug of enchantment a vague disquiet touched her as she became aware of his sexual power over her, but by then it was too late to try to even the balance.

And what followed felt as though the world had ended and then begun all over again, only this time her senses were so heightened—so raw and so feeling and so acute—that she didn't know if she could bear to live with that kind of intensity.

When Keri finally drifted back to some kind of consciousness it was to find Jay dressed—well, half dressed. He was wearing his jeans, his torso bare, the hard, muscular body bathed in moonlight as he stared out of the uncurtained window. He looked like a warrior, she thought—tense, alert and watchful—though what was there to threaten him in the winter sky outside?

He must have sensed that she was awake, because he turned around.

'Hi.'

Did he sound cautious? 'You're dressed,' she observed, stifling a yawn and hoping that she sounded impartial, not needy.

'Yeah. Time I was getting back.' He looked at his watch, as if to illustrate the point. 'It's way past midnight.'

Keri sat up, her hair tumbling down over her naked breasts, seeing the fleeting light of reaction in his eyes—but it was only fleeting. 'But you haven't had anything to eat!'

'This from the woman who doesn't. Ever. Not unless coerced,' he teased. 'Actually, I'm not really hungry.'

But, oddly enough, Keri was—utterly ravenous. She would have liked for him to climb back into bed beside her and for her to go out to the kitchen and pile high a tray full of goodies. They could have eaten them together and he could have fed her again, as he had done so erotically at the house. But maybe that kind of love-play was only part of the wooing, and now that he had no need to woo her he had got straight out of bed and distanced himself. Jay didn't seem to do the cuddling-in-each-other's-arms bit afterwards.

'Could you pass me my robe?'

He pulled a silken-looking Chinese thing from the back of the door and handed it to her, his resolve momentarily wavering when he saw her long, pale limbs emerging from the rumpled sheets like a Venus.

'I'm expecting a call from the States,' he said, by way of explanation—except, of course, that was not the whole story. The kind of sex he'd just shared with Keri was... He shook his head. It took you too close to yourself. Made you feel things you didn't want to feel. If he'd given in to that kind of stuff he could never have done the job he'd been trained for. And he didn't do night-times either, for they brought with them their own particular problems. He felt as if he had strayed into some kind of unknown trap, and he knew he had to get the hell out of there.

She knotted the belt. 'Of course,' she said calmly—amazing, really, considering what was going on inside her head. The woman who had been so thoroughly pleasured now desperately needed to connect. She wanted to run to him, to have him pull her into his arms and show her that what had just taken place in some way mattered.

Wasn't it worth a try?

She walked towards him, leaned forward and kissed him softly, and as she deepened the kiss she felt him respond. But then he drew back, his eyes unreadable, the curve of his mouth regretful—but how true was that? she wondered.

'I have to go, Keri.'

He wanted to go; that was the bottom line. She gave a brittle smile. Sometimes you just had no control over what your face did. 'I'll see you out.'

In silence, they walked towards the hall, where he located his T-shirt and the shirt she had ripped from his back like a hungry animal. Keri as uninhibited predator. It was an image she wasn't used to, and one she wasn't sure she liked very much.

But his parting kiss was almost tender—unless that was hurt female pride searching for the most acceptable interpretation.

'That was incredible,' he said softly.

Mild hysteria made her think she was being marked out of ten. 'Yes, it was.'

'I'll see you tomorrow,' he said.

Somehow she managed the serene kind of grown-up look she knew was expected, even though inside was a little girl who wanted to cling onto his arm and beg him not to leave her. 'You certainly will—unless you can bear to live with only one and a half walls painted.'

Yet the painting seemed somehow irrelevant. Everything did. She bolted the door after he'd gone, with a hand which was trembling, realising that she might be able to lock out his physical presence but that somehow—had she been mad enough to think he wouldn't?—Jay Linur was creeping into her heart.

She slept better than she had anticipated, and by the time she was up and dressed she had talked herself back into a positive attitude. She had no right to blame him because he hadn't met her romantic expectations and spent the night cradled in her arms. If she wanted roses by candlelight then she had picked the wrong man.

She arrived soon after Andy and perched on his desk, sipping coffee.

'Good evening?' he asked casually.

Keri's face didn't react. 'Great,' she answered, non-committally.

The two men were close—had Jay said anything on the lines of *Hey, guess what I'm doing with Keri*? Was that what men did? Especially men who had been close, in an all-male environment where women had their place and not necessarily a very important one. 'How about you?'

'Pretty quiet.' He shrugged. 'Guess I need to get out there and network a little more.'

'Do you miss America?'

He stirred his coffee and shook his head. 'England's been pretty good to me. I like the fact that it's small, that it's surrounded by sea—you feel kind of safe here.'

'But it's not home?' she ventured.

He smiled. 'What's home? Wherever you lay your hat? Well, I must have laid mine in a hundred different places from the age of eighteen until I was almost thirty-two! My parents are dead—my sisters are married and scattered all over. So I guess home is here.'

It wasn't just an insight into Andy's life, but into Jay's as well. He had lived that same nomadic existence, and some people never tired of the excitement of the new and undiscovered. Not just with places, but with people too.

She heard Jay's footfall outside and she tensed. How would he be with her today? Cool? Non-committal? What if...? She felt tiny pinpricks of sweat beading her forehead... What if it was only ever intended to be a one-off? Or a second-off, she amended wryly.

He came in and put his helmet down, took the mail that Andy handed him and headed straight for his office, turning his head very slightly to call over his shoulder.

'Just come in here for a moment, would you, Keri?'

She was being summoned. Her heart racing, she rose to her feet with a certain reluctance, giving Andy what she hoped was a sunny, confident smile, and went towards the inner sanctum.

She stood framed in his doorway and Jay grew hard just thinking about last night.

'Come in,' he said quietly. 'And shut the door behind you.'

For a moment she couldn't move—she felt rooted to the spot, like a tree, and Jay had the power to fell her if he chose.

Keep it businesslike and take the lead from him, she told herself as she quietly closed the door and lifted her eyebrows politely. 'What can I do for you, Jay?'

'You can come right over here and kiss me.'

'I thought we tried that yesterday, and it didn't work.'

'That was before last night.'

'Which surely makes it even more of a bad idea?'

Jay studied her. He had half feared an over-the-top display of emotion—and hadn't a part of him wanted that? Wouldn't that have made it easier to categorise her as being like all the others?

'My, but you're grouchy this morning,' he accused softly.

'Not grouchy at all.'

'Stubborn, then.'

She smiled, feeling more powerful by the moment. 'Because I won't do exactly what you want?'

He laughed. 'I guess.' Deliberately, he ran his eyes slowly over her, from the top of her head to the tip of her toes, blatantly and arrogantly undressing her with his eyes, enjoying the rise of colour and the sudden darkening of her eyes. And enjoying just as much this silent battle of wills. 'Still don't want to kiss me?' he taunted.

'Wanting has nothing to do with it—we've already established that.' She frowned. 'Does Andy know?'

Jay stilled. 'Know *what*, exactly?'

She nearly said, about *us*, but in the nick of time she realised how needlessly possessive that would sound. So she made it as bald as possible—but still a few steps short of how she suspected a SEAL might describe it.

'Does he know we're sleeping together?' It was only after she'd said it that she realised it wasn't strictly accurate.

Jay raised his eyebrows. 'Well, I didn't get on the phone last night after I'd left you to call him, if that's what you mean. And unless you told him before I arrived, then, no.'

'So he doesn't know about the house?'

'You're kidding!' His eyes narrowed. 'How the hell can I expect to have standards about professionalism if I don't adhere to them myself?'

'You bastard,' she said, with feeling. 'I'm sorry I made you flout your higher-than-high standards!'

'Oh, Keri,' he remonstrated softly. 'That wasn't what I meant and you know it! I don't go around boasting about my conquests, if that's what you're asking.'

'I wasn't aware that I *was* a conquest,' she said stiffly.

Hell! 'You're twisting me up with words!' he complained.

'Shall we communicate by sign language then?'

'Or touch?' He rallied instantly, inordinately pleased when he saw a smile curve the corners of her mouth. 'How about we go to a show tonight?'

Keri blinked in surprise. 'What kind of show?'

'Do you like musicals? Because I have two tickets.'

'To what?'

Eyes glittering, he gave the name of a hit which had two Hollywood stars proving their stage credentials and was currently packing them in.

'You can't have tickets for that—they're like gold-dust!'

'Well, I have,' he responded, with cool arrogance. 'So shall I pick you up later? Say around seven? We could go for a drink first, if you like.'

And Keri smiled, something telling her that tonight it *was* safe to have him collect her. The frantic stuff was done—this really was a date.

'Love to,' she said, and hoped that her smile didn't look too soppy.

CHAPTER TWELVE

THE plane bumped down to the sound of spontaneous applause from the passengers and Jay gave a grim smile. It had been a bumpy ride, the aircraft buffeted by storms which had lit the skies with an eerie brilliance. Most people had been terrified, but not him— he'd been on tough flights before, and he knew that if a plane was going to crash then screaming about it wasn't going to stop it.

He'd paid a flying visit to Manchester, summoned there by one of his agents who had been staking out a house which had been sheltering an abducted child caught up in a particularly ugly divorce battle. The police had failed to find her, and in her desperation the mother had contact Linur's.

It had been a delicate and potentially explosive situation, and Jay had gone along to give his man assistance on the sort of case he had once thrived on. There had been both danger and excitement icing the dark, unforgiving night and the long, cold dawn which had followed before they had plucked the child to safety.

But Jay had been aware that his usually sharpened instincts seemed blunted. For once it had been hard to be impartial, to view the case through clear, cold eyes. Instead, he'd found himself identifying with the terror and bewilderment of the child. He'd gone through all the motions, but had felt as if he was only half there—nothing anyone else would have noticed, but he had.

Just as he had noticed Keri's fearful expression when he had told her he was flying north on business.

'What kind of business?' she had asked.

'That's none of *your* business, sweetheart.' He had seen the hurt and worry which had clouded her eyes but had steeled his heart to it. What did she expect? For him to give her a briefing of his case, chapter and verse? And it wasn't just the secrecy, which was vital to the operation, it was her expectation that somehow she had a right to know just because they had something going on between them. Was she planning to pack him sandwiches and tell him to be sure to ring her if he was delayed?

His mouth hardened. It was what women did. They built on relationships and then they worried and fretted about them. Put a woman on a ship full of men, and everything was altered. Inevitably. Women changed the dynamic, and it was both their weakness and their strength. Slowly but surely they sapped the strength of their men with the stealthy allure of domesticity.

Well, he didn't want it. He'd never wanted it. And the sooner she learnt that the better all round—and if she couldn't cope with the situation as it was, rather than how she wanted it to be, then she had better resign herself to the fact that it was over.

There was a text message from her awaiting him. It said. *Come straight round and I'll cook you dinner. K xxx*

His eyes narrowed. He knew what he wanted from her, and it wasn't any damned dinner—just to lose

himself in her body and forget the memory of the human drama he had just dealt with.

When she answered the door, her hair was all over
the place and she looked flustered, but he felt it all the
same—that strong and overpowering need in him she
always provoked.

Her eyes widened. 'Oh, God, is that the time?'

He pulled her into his arms. She smelt of warm milk
and apples. 'Well, hello to you too!'

She gave him a brief, distracted kiss and pulled
away, just as the sound of a child's wail came wafting
through from the sitting room.

Jay froze, memories of the child he had just rescued
playing tricks with his mind, taking him right back to
the cold and the dark and the terror. 'What the hell is
that?'

But she was already dashing along the corridor towards the sound of the wail, calling over her shoulder,
'It's—oh, come through, Jay—it's William.'

He followed her. The wail had become a noisy,
gulping cry, and when he walked into her usually rest-
ful rose-pink room it was almost unrecognisable.
Cushions and crayons littered the floor, the contents
of a fruit dish were scattered all over the sofa, and in
the midst of the general chaos a small child was sobbing against Keri's neck.

She met Jay's eyes over William's silky ebony hair
and gave him a helpless expression. 'Shush, Will,' she
crooned. 'It's all right. Look—here's Jay.'

William turned his head, looked at Jay, and then
screamed even louder before burying his face again.

'He'll be all right in a minute, once he gets to know

you,' she said. 'He's always a bit funny with strangers.'

This must be her nephew, he surmised. Her sister's child. What was he doing here?

'Erin wanted to go for a pedicure,' she explained, as William drummed his feet against her hips.

This explanation fuelled his vague feeling of discontent, and he let it flood in with a sensation of relief. So her sister was getting her toenails painted while her child screamed. Were both of them hostages to beauty, then?

'Why don't you help yourself to a drink?' Keri asked, wondering why his face was looking so thunderous. Surely William's presence wasn't *that* bad? Or was anything bad in Jay's mind if it impeded their journey to the bedroom?

'I don't want a drink,' he said shortly. 'I've had a long night and I'm pretty bushed. Looks like you've got your hands tied here—I'll see you tomorrow.'

He saw her mouth open by a fraction. Her tousled hair fell and mingled with the dark hair of William, who seemed now to be more interested in Jay, for he kept darting him little looks from eyes as ebony-dark as hers. He saw the relaxed way she rested the child on her hip and it was light-years away from the frozen silver model. Her cheeks were all pink, and with the child clinging onto her she looked extremely sexy in a very wholesome way. Who would have dreamed she could do a very credible imitation of an earth mother?

It made him want her even more. But he wanted her to himself and *damn it*—he didn't want to want her this much at all!

'I'll let myself out.'

'Okay, then,' she said faintly, and watched him leave. She couldn't stop the dull sense of foreboding which began to gnaw away at her heart.

Something was happening—he was growing distant from her. But, come to think of it, hadn't there been more and more of that just lately?

She knew she was falling in deep—past the point of no return—but she couldn't seem to do anything about it. On a good day she told herself that there was no reason why she should.

But today was a bad day, for no reason she could think of, and when something was bad it made you dwell on the negative. She settled William on the sofa and he began eating one of the apples which was lying there. She began to pick up all the cushions, her mind fixing and staying on the things which caused her pain if she let them, so she didn't often let them.

Like the fact that Jay had never stayed the night with her. Not once. Even that first night at the house he had left her side while she'd been sleeping.

She hadn't remarked on it at first. Hadn't wanted to scare him or have him think she was getting needy or possessive, though in fact it was neither—she just wanted to hold his strong, warm body during the night and to wake up with him the next day. To touch his face, to outline the strong, firm line of his lips. To make him breakfast and to drink coffee together, just like a normal couple.

But one night, when she had lain back against the pillows with a lazy, satisfied grin just refusing to wipe itself from her face, she had risked it.

'Do you *have* to go, Jay?'

He didn't pause in the act of pulling a sweater over his head. 'I'm afraid so.' There was an odd, fraught kind of silence. 'I do work from home at all kinds of ungodly hours,' he explained tightly. 'The time difference means I can't deal with the States during the day.'

Slowly and deliberately, she sucked the end of her finger and saw his eyes darken.

'And what if I told you I didn't mind being woken up?' she questioned softly.

'I couldn't do it, Keri,' he murmured. 'Think of the trouble I'd be in with your agency if you started to get dark rings underneath your eyes.'

Which was a very neat and diplomatic way of getting out of it, but it hurt.

I'll never ask him again, she had vowed. Ever.

Nor did he ever take her to *his* apartment.

Now, why was that?

But her thoughts were broken by the arrival of Erin, minutes later, her face glowing. 'Oooh, I feel wonderful,' she confided. 'Haven't had that done since...' She bit her lip, but then smiled bravely. 'Well, not for ages, anyway.'

'Who knows?' Keri teased. 'We might even get you to the hairdresser's soon.'

'Steady on!' Erin paused in the middle of buttoning up William's coat and frowned at her twin. 'What's up?'

'Nothing.'

'Keri, it's me you're talking to—remember?'

Keri shrugged. 'Jay just came by.'

Erin looked around. 'So where is he now?'

'He went home.'

'In a grump?'

'What makes you say that?'

'Your face does. Did you have a row?'

'No. No, we haven't had a row.'

'Well, what *is* the matter, Keri?'

Was she fussing over something unnecessary? 'I was just thinking that I've never actually seen where he lives.'

Erin's eyebrows shot up. 'How very peculiar.'

'You think so?'

'Of course I do. Maybe he's shy about asking you.'

'Jay? Shy?' Keri gave a hollow laugh. 'I don't think so!'

'Look, you don't have to be so passive about this, you know. Why don't you call over there and surprise him?'

'No,' Keri said slowly. 'I couldn't.'

Erin looked cross. 'Oh, for goodness' sake, Keri—are you a grown woman or some kind of compliant mouse? What's the worst thing that could happen? He won't let you in?'

But that wasn't the worst thing that could happen. The worst thing was something which haunted her in darker moments, even when she tried not to let it. It all finishing. Jay no longer wanting or needing her. Could the world continue to turn if that should happen? She turned to stare out to where stars twinkled untouchably in the distance. Not her world, that was for sure.

And if it all hinged on whether or not she turned

up unexpectedly at his apartment, then wouldn't it be better to find out now?

She took a cab. He lived in Greenwich, close to the river and the park, and his motorbike stood out from all the expensive cars parked along his street.

Her fingers were trembling as she rang the bell, and when he answered he was wearing just jeans, his hair still damp from the shower, his feet bare, the expression on his face watchful and wary.

'Keri,' he said smoothly. 'What a surprise.'

She stood there and looked at him. She certainly wasn't going to force an entrance.

'Come in.'

'Thank you.'

She walked inside and looked around. The apartment was huge, and had spectacular views of the river, but it was so...so *bare* that it made his office look positively overcrowded. There was essential furniture only—a giant sofa in tough, masculine leather in the sitting room, and a bleached oak dining table with matching chairs in the dining section. There was a frighteningly modern kitchen, which looked like the inside of a spacecraft, and a superb sound system, and that, basically, was that.

It was like his office, only more so, because this was where he *lived*, for heaven's sake. But there was little in the way of decoration, only objects which were useful. It looked, she thought, like a temporary place. As if he was renting and about to leave at any time. Transitory and temporary. As if anyone at all could have been living there, for there was nothing of Jay within its four walls.

'Sit down,' he said. 'Can I get you a drink?'

Unlike him, she didn't refuse. 'Yes, please.'

She sat down on the sofa, leaning back and trying to relax, but feeling about as relaxed as someone on a job interview for a position they really wanted. 'Have you lived here long?'

'Just over a year.' He could see her frowning. 'You like it?'

'I...well, yes. Yes, I do—though it's pretty basic.'

'Well, that's how I like it,' he said.

My, but he was touchy! And she would have had to be the dumbest woman in the world not to read the not-so-subtle warning in *that*.

He opened a bottle of white burgundy, poured out two glasses and handed her one, his mouth softening in a smile. 'I'm cooking some Cajun food—ever tried it before?'

She shook her head and sipped at her wine, impressed yet not surprised at his self-sufficiency. No tin-opener and a can of beans for Jay. 'Never.'

'Then you haven't lived.'

The wine hit her stomach, and by the time he sat her up at the table she realised she was very hungry. He served up a concoction of okra and shrimps and rice, which he called Gumbo.

'Eat,' he said.

She did. It was delicious, and she gave a little moan of greed as she tucked in.

He watched her for a while. 'You're really enjoying it, aren't you?' he observed.

She looked up. 'Don't sound so surprised!'

'But I am. When I first met you, you seemed to have made food your enemy.'

'Well, not any longer! Dinner every night and sandwiches for lunch most days!'

His eyes roved over her. 'You're looking well.'

'If by that you mean I've put on weight, then, yes, I have. I could hardly do up the zip of my jeans this morning.' She put her fork down and recklessly drank another mouthful of wine. 'God only knows what's going to happen when I have to go for my next modelling job!'

The statement hung in the air like a bubble waiting to burst.

'You'll have finished the painting soon,' said Jay carefully.

'That's right.' She certainly couldn't drag it out much longer.

'But you'll carry on modelling?'

He was talking about the future, and suddenly she was scared, but she hid her fear in bravado. 'Of course I will—that's what I do! What did you imagine? That I would set myself up as an interior designer?'

'Why not? You're good.'

'Well, for a start I have no qualifications and very little experience.'

'So what?'

'Because things don't work that way, Jay, that's why not!'

She felt frustrated now, the warmth of the wine evaporating with his words. She was terrified of the job ending, because she didn't know whether she would see him again. He hadn't said, and she was afraid to ask...afraid of what the answer might be.

'You've stopped eating,' he said softly.

Well, damn him! Damn him for his indifference and his stubborn determination not to let her spend the night with him!

Keri pushed the plate away, stretched her arms high above her head and yawned. 'I'm tired too,' she confessed.

He watched while the T-shirt spread tightly across her breasts, their tips outlined in provocative display with the dark glossy hair spilling down all over them. He knew what she was doing. It was a blatant demonstration of her physical power over him. For a few moments he had a silent tussle with himself. So, did he give in? Sometimes he liked to deny himself, just to feel fully in control. To prove he could. And it would certainly make it easier. If he made love to her now, he could hardly ask her to leave...

But if she stayed, then where was that going to lead? To more nights, and then still more? Soon she would be cluttering up his very masculine bathroom with all kinds of feminine junk and leaving drifts of lace underwear everywhere. Then she would start asking him what time he was coming home and keeping tabs on him. Very soon after that they would be shopping at the supermarket together—dithering over which brand of juice to buy—and wouldn't that be a kind of living hell?

'Come here,' he instructed silkily.

There was something in his expression which made it impossible to disobey him, even if she had wanted to. And some new, hard light in his eyes, both cautioning and yet inviting.

Like a robot she got up and went to sink onto his lap, but he shook his head.

'No. Not yet.' His eyes glittered. 'First of all, take your clothes off.'

Keri blinked. 'Just like that?'

'Wouldn't you like to strip for me, Keri?' His voice hardened. 'I thought that was what you were working up to.'

Some feeling like fear tiptoed down her spine. He was making her feel like... Like what? Like a live exhibit? A good-time girl? She looked at him, shaken. 'Oddly enough, no. I wouldn't.'

He raised his eyebrows, but in his heart he knew he had been testing her. Now she was hurt; that much was plain. And it told him something that maybe he had been blind to, or had maybe simply chosen not to see. That she saw more in what they had than just a very enjoyable affair. And, if they continued it, wouldn't she get hurt even more? That was his track record, after all—causing pain to women because he couldn't give them what they really wanted.

But he saw the tremble of her lips and something inside him melted. If fighting it didn't seem to work, he found he didn't even want to. He reached out to pull her down onto his lap, because the physical act was easy—he could lose himself in that and forget all the troublesome questions which nagged at his mind.

'Kiss me,' he whispered.

For a moment she resisted, was ice in his arms, but

he drifted his mouth to her neck and the thaw began and there was nothing she could do to stop it.

Her eyes fluttered to a close. 'Oh, Jay,' she said weakly, hating that weakness even while his hands began to stroke her into molten submission.

He took her to his bedroom and took her clothes off himself, slowly—agonisingly slowly—kissing her flesh as he laid it bare.

And she tiptoed her fingers down over his torso, down over his hips, and down further still...

'Keri,' he groaned.

'What?' This was better. The cold-eyed man had gone, and in his place was someone who could be as weak as she was. He loved to control—well, now let *him* be controlled.

She wriggled from beneath him and slithered down his body, her tongue sliding its way to his belly, loving the way he squirmed, holding himself tense, as if he couldn't quite believe that she was going to...

'Oh, God—yes!' he moaned.

She had never done it to a man before, not even with Jay, but she just followed her instincts, her mouth gentle, caressing, teasing and inciting. She found what he liked and then she did it some more. And then some more.

And when at last he moved to push her head away she wouldn't let him. She wanted to possess that most essential part of him in a way which made her feel almost primitive as she tasted the salt which was present in blood and sweat and tears, too.

He shuddered, lost in the mists of pleasure and, for a moment, totally vulnerable.

He lifted her off him and flipped her over onto her back, moving to lie above her, his eyes glittering with a hectic green-grey light, his expression unreadable. She was going to stay in his bed all night, he realised.

'Your turn now,' he said, in an odd kind of voice.

CHAPTER THIRTEEN

JAY seemed edgy and distracted when they showered and dressed to go to work the following morning, and it was obvious that he felt relieved when she went off to find a cab on her own, though he did his best to hide it.

And while Keri floated around in a dream, because they'd finally spent the night together, Jay remained on edge for the rest of the day. When he told her that he needed to 'catch up' that evening, she wasn't really surprised. Hurt, yes, but not surprised. But neither of them had slept much the night before, and things would be back to normal tomorrow.

But next morning it looked particularly bleak, with a dank drizzle leaking down from dark and heavy clouds.

The rain was seeping into Keri's face as she pulled her bag over her shoulder and ran up the steps, and once inside she looked around, as if recognising for the first time that the end of the job really was in sight.

It was amazing the difference she had made—transforming the place into somewhere unrecognisable from the bland and dingy building it had been. The strong, vibrant colours had worked out even better than she had anticipated. The rich sapphire hue emphasised and reflected the living water outside, and the dimensions of the rooms were dramatic enough to take it.

Even Jay had said so.

'Some people lack the ability to see what possibilities a place can have,' he had murmured. 'And you have that ability. It's a gift, Keri. It looks so different.

Maybe he would let her buy a few more prints. She could find a few posters of New Orleans, maybe. He had spent his first few years there and he liked cooking Cajun food—what could be better?

Perhaps she could even get away with a large, leafy plant in the corner—weren't all places supposed to have living things in them? He might like living in a place which resembled an interrogation cell, but that didn't mean he had to work in one.

Andy was on the phone, and she was just hanging up her dripping raincoat and wondering what Jay's reaction would be to a soothing and therapeutic fish tank, when he hung up and looked at her.

'Hi, Keri,' he said, just a little too casually.

Something told her something was wrong.

'Has something happened?'

'Depends what you mean by happened,' answered Andy carefully.

Keri had grown to like Andy. He had a relaxed and uncomplicated nature—so why was he looking as though he had sat down in a nest of ants?

'Where's Jay?'

He took a deep breath, like someone who had been rehearsing how to say something. Or maybe how he had been told to say it.

'He's gone.'

'Gone? Gone where?'

'He had to fly out to New York this morning.'

'How long for?'

'He didn't say.' He must have seen something stricken in her face, because he added, 'It wasn't planned, Keri.'

Keri stared sightlessly at the ground. Maybe it hadn't been—but there were phones, weren't there? And texts. Why, you could even send an e-mail from an airport these days. But Jay hadn't, and it wasn't difficult to work out why.

And there was that soft, underlying note of something approaching sympathy in Andy's voice too.

She looked up. 'You know, don't you, that I've been seeing him? Did he tell you?'

He shook his head. 'He never discusses his personal life with me—ever. I worked it out for myself.' He gave her a sweet smile. 'When a couple go to such a lot of trouble to avoid being together then there's usually a reason why.'

Yes, they had avoided each other as much as possible at work—at *Jay's* instigation—but when she stopped to think about it he had managed to avoid too much contact all round, hadn't he? Never sleeping with her apart from that one reluctant night.

Had Keri committed the cardinal female crime of wishing for something and then imagining that it was coming true? She had wanted him to feel something deeper for her, as she had for him, but it was patently obvious that he didn't.

Andy patted her hand, like a man making peace and

offering comfort. 'It isn't personal, you know. It's just the way he is.'

Her eyes were very clear and bright. 'And what way is that?'

He took a deep breath, as if weighing up whether or not to tell her, but maybe something resolute and determined in her eyes made him decide. 'This is what he does, Keri. He won't be owned or possessed or constrained. He's a free spirit, and the moment he thinks he's in danger of being tied down, or tying *himself* down,' he amended hastily, 'then he just cuts and runs.'

'Runs from what?' she asked tonelessly. 'Himself?'

'Who knows? Maybe.' He was quiet for a moment. 'Let me tell you something about him. I've known him a long time, and he was the best damn commander I ever had, but even I sometimes feel I don't really know him. He's tough and cold and emotionally detached, and he needed to be. Those kind of men make the best leaders.'

He glanced up at her. 'When I left the SEALs I sort of…well, I went off the rails. A lot of the guys can't cope with the reality of the real world, and I was one of them. I started drinking—big-time—and then… well, someone thought that it might be a good idea to introduce an already screwed-up guy to drugs.'

His eyes narrowed, and Keri saw the pain in them.

'When Jay found me again I was pretty much dead—I sure wasn't living. He picked me up and cleaned me up and told me that if I ever so much as looked at a chemical substance again he would deal with me himself, and I believed him.'

His voice changed and his eyes looked startlingly blue as he looked into hers. 'I never looked back,' he said. 'He gave me a job—and then somehow he swung it for me to come and work over here when he was starting up. And I worked my butt off, because I wanted to show him just how much I owed him. My life, really,' he added simply.

Keri nodded, for a moment her sense of admiration for her lover eclipsing her bitterness that he had gone away so abruptly.

'He *rescues* people, Keri,' said Andy. 'That's what he does. He sees what they need and he gives it to them, and then he moves on.'

It was like being given the answer to a conundrum which had been puzzling you for ages.

He rescued people.

Yes, of course he did.

He had swept in and rescued Keri, first from the snow and then from her sexual desert, topping it all off by encouraging her to start using her own creative talents instead of just being the blank canvas a model invariably was.

That he had failed to complete the fantasy by galloping off on his charger with her firmly in the saddle didn't mean that *he* had failed, only that she had failed to understand him. Or refused to.

She nodded, like someone who had just been given a piece of bad news but who was determined not to go to pieces over it.

'Well, I guess I'd better finish what I'm being paid for.' Her smile was as bright as anything she had ever flashed on camera. 'And don't I get any coffee this morning, Andy Baxter?'

She told Erin about it between tears and sips of wine. 'God, I could do with a cigarette!' she wailed.

'Well, you can't have one,' said Erin firmly. 'You gave up years ago and you're not starting again now.' She tipped some more wine into her glass. 'Maybe it's not over,' she said hopefully.

But, in a way, wasn't that the worst possible scenario? Nothing would change except for her feelings. Jay wouldn't—why should he? He was happy with his life the way it was. Being a free spirit was probably very enjoyable.

But Keri's feelings would grow—she just knew they would—and where would that get her?

'It has to be over,' she said, putting the glass down with a bump. 'I need it to be, for my peace of mind.'

'And if he calls—you're going to tell him that?'

There was a pause. Keri looked at her twin. 'Well, I was actually hoping that *you* might do that.'

There was a short, disbelieving pause and then Erin shook her head. 'Oh, no, Keri—you have to be out of your mind!'

'Please, Erin, please—we used to do it for each other when we were younger, so what's the difference?'

'Are you serious? The difference is time, and maturity. For a start, I'm ten pounds heavier.'

'I wouldn't count on that at the moment,' Keri answered wryly. 'And you could wear a big sweater!'

Erin looked furious. 'For God's sake, Keri—you've

had a sexual relationship with this man! What am I supposed to do when he starts coming on to me? I presume he knows you have a twin?'

Keri nodded.

'Well, how long do you think it will take him to guess it isn't you at all? About a second?'

Keri frowned. Maybe she was right. Jay might be insensitive to a woman's needs, but he certainly wasn't insensitive to her desires—not only would he guess, but he would be furious!

Did she care about his rage?

No, she did not.

'We could set a meeting up in a restaurant,' she said pleadingly. 'A busy restaurant, where there's no chance of him so much as touching you—he hates public displays of affection anyway. You can tell him over the first course, then walk out and leave him to pay the bill—it will be so short and businesslike that he won't have time to guess it isn't me.'

'Tell him *what*, exactly?'

'That you don't want to see him again. You don't even have to explain yourself, Erin—he certainly didn't offer me any explanation about why he left without so much as a goodbye. And it's only *if* he rings,' she added. 'Which he may not even do. I'm out of his office now, so probably out of his life. This may be the way he's using to break it off without having to go through the discomfort of telling me.'

There was silence for a moment, and when Erin spoke her face was very serious.

'Why can't you just do that yourself—tell him?'

Admission time—time to tell the truth, even though

it damned her. 'Because I don't think I can resist him,' she confessed in a hollow whisper. 'Maybe I won't even want to resist him. But I have to—I need to. If he makes love to me and persuades me to stay it's only putting off the inevitable and increasing the likelihood of more pain. Erin, please. Please.'

There was another pause.

'My hair is different from yours.'

Keri smiled, and the look she gave her sister was tender. 'I think you've done all your mourning now, don't you, kiddo?' she said softly. 'And I know that my hairdresser would be over the moon if you let him style your hair. A present from me to you—as a kind of thank-you for doing something I'm too cowardly to do myself. Think how great you felt when I persuaded you to get your toes done!'

Anticipation gleamed from her eyes and Erin's mouth twitched into an answering smile. 'A baggy jumper, you say? It'll have to be a pretty downmarket restaurant!'

Jay put his helmet down and looked around his office, surveying the bright prints, the warm and vibrant walls, and some tall, fleshy plant which made the room seem somehow alive. He frowned. He didn't remember there being a plant there.

He walked over to the window and stared out at where the sunlight was dancing over the water. His business in New York had been necessary, but not urgent, but he had needed to get away. A change of scene, a change of people—he had never known it not to work before, but this time it hadn't.

So what had gone wrong?

New York had been buzzing, and it was a city he knew well—yet the refuge he had sought had seemed somehow empty.

He had been haunted by Keri, picturing her wide, dark eyes last thing at night, and every morning he had woken aching, unable to dispel the feeling that maybe this time he had cut and run too soon, that he had let go of something which was precious, only he had failed to see it at the time.

'Where is she?' he demanded.

Andy handed him a coffee. 'Who?' he questioned innocently.

'Who? Keri, of course,' Jay growled.

'The job's finished, boss. She's gone.'

'Gone?' he echoed blankly.

So they had got the place back to themselves at last. By rights, he should be pleased. He could work in peace now, and not be distracted by a foxy woman in paint-splattered overalls. He frowned. 'What did she say?'

'Not a lot. She's billed you for the work owing—you'll find it on your desk.'

Jay walked into his office, found the envelope sitting on his desk and slit it open.

But inside was a bill—just that, nothing more. No little note saying, Hope you like it. No kisses. Nothing.

What the hell did you expect?

He picked up the phone and rang her, and it rang for such a long time that he was waiting for it to go through to the machine when she answered at last.

'Hello?'

'Keri?'

Her heart pounded. Keep calm, she told herself. 'Jay?'

'Yes.' He smiled. 'Missed me?'

She quashed the desire to say *Why did you leave without telling me?* She wasn't going to show her hurt, or show she cared. She had no right to say that, in any case—he had never promised her anything. 'I've been busy,' she prevaricated. 'Doing some magazine work.'

'Oh? Anything interesting?'

'Advertising stockings, actually,' she said matter-of-factly.

Stockings? He very nearly dropped the phone. 'So when am I going to see you?'

He had gone away without telling her, and now he was back and clearly feeling rampant. This could obviously be a sexual relationship made in heaven—but was that enough? No, it was not.

Her nerve nearly failed her, but she told herself that it was better this way. Better to suffer the ache of missing him now instead of rekindling the embers of something which was dying.

When something came to an end there had to be some kind of closure—she just didn't trust herself to go through with it on her own.

She looked down at her diary; he wasn't to know that the pages were blank. 'How about lunch? Tomorrow?'

'Lunch?' he echoed, surprised.

'You don't have a problem with lunch, do you?' Of course he did. He probably wanted to carry her straight off to bed, and if he was only just back then he would be needed in the office.

Jay shook his head. He wanted to see her now. Or tonight. And he knew he had no right to ask. He could hear the slight coolness in her voice and knew that he deserved it.

'I can do lunch,' he agreed. 'Where?'

She closed her eyes as she gave him the name of the restaurant. God forgive me, she thought, but I have to do it this way.

CHAPTER FOURTEEN

THERE was a slight murmur in the restaurant, and Jay's eyes moved in her direction as she walked in.

His weren't the only ones, but that shouldn't have surprised him. She really was very, very beautiful, but it was rare for him to observe her from afar like this. He watched her weave her way through the busy room. And his eyes narrowed.

She walked over towards his table, her fingers gripping onto her clutch-bag. 'Hi.'

'Hi,' he said softly.

She sat down. Her hands were trembling, he noticed, and he scanned her eyes, but it was difficult to read anything in them—she'd gone overboard on the make-up and that damned fringe was flopping about all over the place.

She cleared her throat. 'Before we go any further, there's something I need to say to you, Jay.'

He had been watchful before, but now an extra sense of perception crept in and his thumb moved thoughtfully to rub at the faint rasp of shadow at his jaw. 'You don't want to order a drink first?'

'No.' She shook her head, the dark hair spilling like ebony satin all over her shoulders. 'I haven't come here for a drink. Not even for lunch—not really.'

'How very intriguing. What have you come for, then?'

He could see the nervous flutter of her lashes.

'It's not easy to say…'

'Oh, do try,' he coaxed, an odd kind of note in his voice. 'I'm fascinated.'

'I…I just wanted to tell you how much I enjoyed what we had. But I've been doing a lot of thinking— and, well, I think it's best if we don't see one another again.' She gave a brittle smile. 'That's it, really.' And pushed her chair back. 'I shouldn't think you'll be *too* broken-hearted.'

He waited until she was standing, and then he smiled.

'Will you do me a favour before you go?' he asked quietly.

She looked startled. 'What is it?'

His voice became edged with a certain hardness. 'Just tell Keri I'll be in touch.'

Keri had thought of leaving the Ansaphone on. Of vacating her apartment for a week or two. Even of ringing her agency up and asking if they had any lengthy shoots in exotic locations.

But what would be the point? If Jay wanted to see her, then see her he would—she didn't doubt that for a moment. And, though her courage had failed her before, surely she could grasp it with two hands now? He knew what she wanted—or, rather, what she *needed* to do, and he was man enough to accept that.

When the doorbell rang, loudly and angrily, she didn't need to check in the peephole to see who it was. She just opened the door to him, thinking how tight his features looked. He was dressed in his habitual black, but today he looked as menacing as she had ever seen him.

'You'd better come in.'

He was silent as he stepped inside, silent as he closed the door behind him. His eyes were hot and angry, and when he spoke his voice was as tight as a coiled spring.

'Do you take me for a complete fool, Keri?'

She was taken aback by the depth of his venom. 'How did you guess?'

'How did I guess?' he exploded. 'That you'd sent your twin to try to do your dirty work for you? Do you think I'm completely lacking in comprehension?'

'But we're identical!' she blurted out.

'No, you look nearly the same,' he corrected grimly. 'But you are *not* identical. No two human beings are— nor ever could be. For a start you're a model, and you have a way of moving which is both studied and natural—your sister doesn't. She talks differently. She clearly *thinks* differently too. I've never seen a woman look more uncomfortable—tell me, did you have to twist her arm to get her to agree?'

Keri turned and began walking away, but Jay followed her, and once they had reached the sitting room there was no escape left to her. He caught her, turned her round to face him, the grey-green eyes blazing.

'Did you?'

'Yes,' she admitted, in a whisper.

'Why, Keri? Just tell me why! If you want it to be over, then why the hell didn't you tell me so yourself? You're a strong woman—an independent woman—

surely you must have had to say that to men plenty of times during your life?'

She bit her lip. In this he was wrong. She wasn't strong—not around him. She was all open and raw and hurting, weak and wounded from the pain of wanting him.

'Don't make me say it, Jay!'

'Say what? That you've had enough? That your rough-tough man was good for a while but now he's shown you that you're a normal woman who can experience pleasure it's time to move on to someone more suited to a high-class model?'

The way he said *high-class* made it sound like something else altogether.

'Don't be so dense!' she snapped. 'It isn't like that, and you bloody well know it!'

Jay expelled a breath. His heart was pounding like a piston and he wanted to shake her and kiss her all at the same time. What the *hell* was she doing to him? 'Then tell me what it *is* like, Keri?' he demanded silkily.

'*You're* the one who just upped and went off without even telling me you were going! You're the cautious, wary man who goes on about your independence and the way you like *your* flat to look. As if I'm trying to ensnare you and get you to march me down the aisle!'

'This is all to do with the fact that I went away on business without first asking your permission?'

'That's got nothing to do with it! You were running away!'

He froze and stared at her incredulously. 'I was *what*? And just what, pray, was I running away from?'

'From me! From the relationship! Just the way you always do. Andy told me.'

'Oh, did he?' he questioned dangerously. 'Well, I'll just have to have a word with Andy—he works with me, for God's sake, he's not my damned analyst!'

'Oh, don't shoot the messenger!' she declared furiously. 'I didn't actually need Andy to tell me, if you must know. I'd worked it out for myself and he just confirmed it. Well, I've made it easy for you. I'm giving you the let-out clause. It's over! That's what you want, isn't it?'

There was silence for a moment, and when he looked at her his eyes were bright and piercing. 'Is that what you want?'

Of course it wasn't what she wanted! She glared at him. 'I asked first!'

He felt a pain so fierce he couldn't believe that it wasn't physical. 'Oh, Keri,' he groaned. 'Of course it isn't what I want.'

She didn't care if it scared him away; she just knew that she could not exist in this curious half-life of not knowing. 'Then just what *do* you want, Jay?' she asked pointedly.

He knew he owed her this, but it was difficult to find the words to describe the way he felt—he'd never had to do it before. Not even to himself. Yet he looked into her dark eyes and knew he had to. No, he wanted to. He just wasn't sure he knew how.

Just when had this all happened? he asked himself dazedly. This connection to another person which seemed to have reached out and captured him? In his time he had triumphed in hostage rescue and guerrilla warfare, but this was completely unknown territory.

'I want you,' he said at last.

There should have been joy, but all she felt was suspicion. And feelings which she had been flattening down, as you would a sandcastle, suddenly erupted out in a storm.

'Sure you do, Jay—that's why you ran away. Because I had the temerity to turn up uninvited at your apartment and end up staying the night with you! My God, you couldn't have given me a clearer message if you'd tried!'

He sighed. 'I know.'

It was the first chink she had ever seen in his armour. A fleeting moment of something which, if it were any other man than Jay, might almost be described as vulnerability. And all her anger left her. She felt as cautious as someone trying to offer food to a wild, starving animal.

Her voice softened. 'So why? What's changed?'

'I have,' he said slowly. 'I've changed—or, rather, you've made me want to change. I've never wanted to settle down before, and I always ran away from commitment because…'

He could blame a lot of things; that was what people did. His parents' divorce and the subsequent transatlantic ping-pong. Or his choice of a male-dominated career and his need for the emotional detachment which that career demanded.

Or he could say it how it was. Incredibly and unbelievably how it was. So simple, really, like all the very best things in life.

He looked at her, and she had never seen his eyes look so bright. 'Because I never found the right woman before, and now I have.'

For a moment she didn't believe him. Didn't dare to for fear that she was dreaming it and in a moment she would wake up to the bleak reality of a life without Jay. But the message burning from his eyes told her that he spoke the truth, plain and simple. He cared for her. Deeply. Deeper than deep. He hadn't yet used the conventional vocabulary for saying so, but then Jay was not a conventional man. And love didn't always have to be spoken out loud.

Some women might have wanted more than that, but she took the words at more than their face value. He was breaking what for him was a taboo. He had started searching beneath what was happening on the surface of his life, and for a man like Jay that was something pretty big.

Those other words might follow, but she wanted to savour this—the look in his eyes which was reaching out to her, telling her that this strong, experienced man could be vulnerable too.

Come to think of it, she felt a bit that way herself. As if she was standing on the brink of a great big sea, and was about to dabble her toe in and get it wet.

'Oh, Jay,' she whispered.

Some day he would tell her about the bitter transatlantic custody battle which had dominated his growing up. And of the fear of making any place too permanent, knowing that the courts could snatch him

away at any time. Through all his childhood he had
never trusted in the word 'home'.

He held his arms out and she went into them, as if
she had found her safe harbour too, and they stood
there together for a long, long time.

CHAPTER FIFTEEN

THE light had that bright, almost bleached quality which was particular to the Caribbean. Huge, fleshy palm trees fringed the dancing aquamarine of the sea and provided welcome shade from the dazzling sun overhead.

The photo-shoot was finished, and the other models and stylists and photographers were paying serious attention to the cocktails on offer at the beach bar, but Keri felt light-headed after one and a half Cosmopolitans. It was really too hot to drink alcohol, and she wished she could just find herself on a plane heading back to England.

And Jay.

'Think I'll head back to the hotel.' She yawned. 'Maybe have a sleep and then go for a swim.'

No one could persuade her to change her mind, and she didn't think they'd miss her much. Something happened to a woman when she was in love and the object of her affections was several thousand miles away. It meant she was there only in body and not in spirit, no matter how much she tried.

Over the months something had changed in her too, because time changed everything. Her feelings for Jay had grown deeper and stronger—the tiny pebble on which their relationship had started had become a firm bedrock. They lived their lives in parallel harmony—

each with their successful career, spending nights and weekends together in his flat or hers.

She glanced out at the pale blue water. Was there something inherent in human nature that made you always long for what you didn't have? She had the relationship she had always longed for—one that fulfilled her in every way which mattered—and yet somehow she wanted more. She wanted marriage, she realised—and babies too. And, while he showed her that he adored her in every way that counted, she sensed that the whole family package would be a commitment too far.

So stop yearning for the impossible, she told herself—just enjoy what you have.

She saw a figure in the far distance, heading her way, and her idle glance became a double-take as her heart suddenly missed a beat. She shook her head slightly. For a minute there she had imagined she'd seen Jay, walking across the beach towards her.

Yeah, sure. He had secretly taken a flight out to join her the day before she was due to fly home—in your dreams, Keri!

She continued to walk towards the approaching man, waiting for confirmation that it was just another tall, dark stranger enjoying the delights of a Caribbean holiday.

It was difficult to say at what point she realised that she had not been mistaken. She was too far away to see the expression on the beautiful scarred face, and his eyes were shielded by a pair of wraparound shades, but some sense which transcended sight told her without a doubt that it was Jay.

She was so taken aback that her footsteps faltered to a halt. Funny how reality never quite fitted the dream. She should be flinging her arms out and running towards him, and he should catch her in his arms and whirl her round and round and round. But...

Why was he here?

She looked, he thought, like the stuff that dreams were made of, silhouetted against the blinding light in some pale, floaty dress with a flower-laden straw hat shielding her face from the blazing sun.

He moved towards her slowly, wanting to enjoy the moment, his heart beating loud and strong in his chest, his head feeling curiously light. Now he could see the pale heart-shaped face, and the look of bewilderment and anxiety in the dark eyes, and he felt a rush of something deeper than desire.

'What's happened?' Keri demanded, her heart beating with fear. 'What are you doing here?'

He smiled. 'What kind of a greeting is that for your lover?'

Briefly, she thought how modern, how *temporary* that sounded. She looked up at him questioningly, but she could not read the expression behind the shades he wore and it was too blindingly bright to ask him to take them off. 'Jay?'

He reached his hand out, brushing the fringe from her eyes as he had once done a lifetime ago. 'Aren't you pleased to see me?' he asked softly.

'Of course I am,' she answered breathlessly, but she didn't fall into his arms, and neither did he pull her into them. 'Nothing's wrong, is it?'

'Well, that depends on your definition of wrong.'

'*Jay!*' Her voice was shaking, remonstrating, breathless. 'I'm due home tomorrow—why are you here?'

'Because I've missed you.'

'Well, that's…'

'That's what?'

'Surprising,' she admitted.

'Yeah,' he agreed, with a rueful smile. 'Thought I'd be crazy about a woman who gave me plenty of space.'

She opened her eyes very wide. She had clung on to her independence like a lifeline, because an independent woman was the one he had been attracted to.

'And aren't you?'

'Completely and utterly crazy,' he said gravely.

'It doesn't happen very often,' she pointed out. 'The trips, I mean.'

'No.'

'And you spent your whole life travelling all over the place.'

'I know I did.' And he hoped to God that she wasn't living the kind of life he had lived when he was in the SEALs! No, he knew she wasn't—she was sweet and loyal and true—but when she was away he found himself aching for her in a way which was quite alien to him. But if that was the way she wanted it, then that was the way it had to be. He bent and touched her lips with his. 'Do you like being away for weeks at a time, sweetheart?'

Keri hesitated. 'Well, actually, no—not really.'

He frowned. 'Then why do you do it?'

'Because it's my job! Because the best shoots are

ones like these—they pay well and keep my profile high. And, oddly enough, I seem to have got more work since I developed a few curves—and that's all down to you, Jay!'

'But what happened to the interior design?' he questioned. 'I thought my offices were supposed to be your starting block for a whole new change of direction?'

'That was more *your* dream, not mine!'

'I thought for a while it was yours, too, Keri. Did exposure to it put you off it?'

She bit her lip. Oh, what the hell? Just tell him—*tell him.* 'I decided not to start something else because my relationship with you was too new and too important, and I wanted to concentrate on that. I didn't want to make any big career changes because I didn't...' Her voice faltered and her words trailed away as she stared down at the sand.

'Didn't what?' he prompted softly. 'Look at me, Keri.'

This was the crunch moment. Did she have the courage to say it and risk the consequences?

'I can't see your eyes,' she whispered.

He took the shades off. 'How's that?' he questioned steadily.

Better—and worse. She had never seen him look more intent or serious, and she knew then that she had no choice, that the crunch time really *had* come.

'I didn't know if we were going to last. Or if you would change your mind about commitment,' she admitted. 'And I wasn't sure that I could cope with all that if I'd made a huge life-change.'

He nodded, recognising that insecurity still dogged

her. She hadn't rushed him, or pushed him or hinted or cajoled—and hadn't part of him perhaps been waiting for her to do that, wondering if then he truly would feel trapped? But this relationship was no trap. He had found a place he wanted to stay and he wanted to secure that place, to make it permanent and to make it home. To anchor down. And he needed to tell her.

'I love you, Keri,' he said simply, wondering why it had taken so long for him to get around to saying it. He felt as if someone had lit a fire inside him. It had started out as just a tiny flicker, the kind of flame you had to cherish and to nurture, and now it was blazing within him. And feelings, he was discovering, like fires, couldn't be hurried. 'I love you,' he said again, and his smile was blinding.

'Oh, Jay!' She began to cry, and he pulled her into his arms and held onto her as if he would never let her go. After a while she was through, and he kissed the tip of her nose.

'What the hell are you crying about?' he questioned tenderly.

'I love you too, so much!'

By now he had learnt that women *always* cried for a reason, and if Keri was crying her heart out because she loved him, then that was just fine with him.

Everything seemed to happen in a bit of a blur after that. They kissed for a while, and quite passionately too—but they were on a Caribbean beach where that kind of behaviour was seen as perfectly respectable, so nobody gave them a second glance.

Until eventually Keri just wanted some privacy.

'Shall we go back to the hotel?'

He smiled and felt the pump of his heart. 'I guess we'd better.'

They walked hand in hand along the sand, but as they approached the hotel they heard the jubilant beat of steel drums and saw a couple barefoot in the sea, the woman dressed in white with a garland of flowers in her hair and the man in a white tuxedo.

'Oh, Jay, look,' she breathed. 'It's a wedding!'

He thought fleetingly that it was easier to get behind enemy lines than to understand what was going on inside the head of a woman. 'You want to get married?' he questioned casually. 'Here?'

She stopped, dead. 'Oh, my God! You want to marry me?'

'Of course I do,' he answered steadily. 'What do you think I came out here for? Do you want to marry me?'

'You know I do! But not here,' she said firmly. 'I mean, I know it's beautiful and romantic and everything, but...' She looked up at him and her eyes were suddenly anxious. 'I'd really like my parents there. And Erin—she'd never forgive me if I did it without telling her. Would you mind, darling?'

He thought of Keri's twin—of her courage and her strength and the little boy she was raising just fine.

His face softened as he tilted up her chin to look at him. 'Tell you what—how do you suppose your family would like a holiday in the Caribbean?'

And in that moment she loved him so much she felt her heart would burst. 'Oh, Jay! Can't you just imagine William playing on that beautiful sand?'

He nodded and drew a deep breath, knowing that

he couldn't put this off any longer. 'There's something else, Keri.'

Some unrecognisable quality in his voice made her look at him very hard.

'You see, my name isn't Jay Linur at all.'

EPILOGUE

KERI gave the ribbon around the ceramic pot holding a bay tree a last tweak, and stood back for an overall view of the newly painted shop-front. The opening of Linur Lifestyles was due to take place in a couple of hours' time. There were bottles of champagne chilling, and soon caterers would be arriving with bite-sized hamburgers and mini fish and chips housed in tiny little cornets of newspaper. 'A celebration of the best of both English and American cuisine,' Keri had announced, and Jay had laughed.

'What do you think?' she asked now, anxiously.

He looked down at her. 'Honestly?'

'Honestly.'

He smiled. 'I think it looks absolutely incredible. And so, incidentally, do you. But then, you always do.'

She smiled back as she touched his face, remembering the bombshell he had dropped just before their wedding. About his father, heir to one of America's biggest fortunes, which Jay had inherited. 'Just too much money,' he had said bitterly. 'And that kind of wealth taints things.' He had wanted good to come of it, not corruption, and had set up a charitable foundation to help children who were underprivileged in all senses of the word. And he had adopted his mother's surname to distance himself from all of the expectation which his father's carried.

Had she been shocked by the revelation? Not really, no. Nothing Jay did could surprise her—only delight her. She had thought right at the beginning that learning to know him was like peeling away all the layers of an onion, and in that she had been uncannily right.

Oh, he could still be autocratic, and stubborn, and high-handed, but these days she found that a bit of a turn-on. Well, more than a bit.

He lifted her hand from where it was still tweaking unnecessarily at the ribbon and lifted it to his lips. It was a sweet and romantic gesture, but then he captured her gaze as he slowly licked his way along one of the fingers and Keri coloured with pleasure. Gone was the man who had only shown affection in bed—but then, so much had changed.

With Jay. With her. With them both. Love was a liberating thing, she decided—it made you free to say what was really in your heart, instead of worrying whether or not it was the right thing to say. And the astonishing thing was that their wants and their needs seemed to coincide perfectly.

It had all started with a remark he had made while they were waiting for the papers to come through for their Caribbean wedding. They had been strolling along a moon-washed beach, with the stars as bright as diamonds in the sky above them.

'The stars are so clear here,' Jay had said, almost wistfully, and she'd remembered him saying something similar before—that city lights meant you couldn't really see the stars properly.

And so she had hatched a plan. They would move to the country and he could work from an office there, leaving Andy in charge of the London office.

'I really think he's ready for promotion,' she had

said seriously. 'Ready to move out from underneath your wing. And I think it's time you stopped doing such dangerous missions.'

'Oh, do you?' He laughed, thinking that once he would have been outraged if anyone had suggested that. But now he was ready. More than ready.

'Yes. And I can quit modelling—I *want* to, Jay—and I can start up the design business. I can afford to.'

'*We* can afford to,' he said possessively.

Keri nodded, growing warm with pleasure because it all seemed to make such perfect sense.

'And I can give my apartment to Erin, and I'm not going to take no for an answer. She can live there or she can sell it, if that's what she wants.'

Erin had agreed to accept the gift, bowing under the gentle pressure from both Keri and Jay. In the end she had opted to sell, and to move to the country not far from them.

'There's not a lot of point me being in London if you're not there, Keri,' she'd said. 'That's if you don't mind, Jay?'

He'd shaken his head. 'I don't mind a bit.'

Jay had grown to understand the intense bond between the twins, to cherish it and not to be threatened by it, as some men might have been. And he liked Erin—she was a lot like his wife, but she was different. As he'd said—no two people were the same, even though a lot of people seemed to have difficulty telling them apart. But he would have known Keri in the dark from a hundred paces, and that was just instinct.

No, maybe not just instinct. It was something else—something much stronger than instinct.

He smiled down at his wife.

It was love.

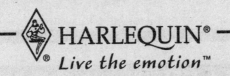

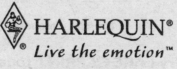

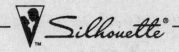

SPECIAL EDITION™

Emotional, compelling stories that capture the intensity of living, loving and creating a family in today's world.

Desire

Modern, passionate reads that are powerful and provocative.

nocturne

Dramatic and sensual tales of paranormal romance.

Romantic SUSPENSE

Romances that are sparked by danger and fueled by passion.

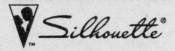